THE UNWANTED AMISH TWIN

A STAND-ALONE AMISH ROMANCE NOVEL

SAMANTHA PRICE

Copyright © 2023 by Samantha Price

All rights reserved.

No part of this book may be reproduced in any form or by any electronic or mechanical means, including information storage and retrieval systems, without written permission from the author, except for the use of brief quotations in a book review.

This book is a work of fiction. Any resemblance to any person, living or dead, is purely coincidental. The personal names have been invented by the author, and any likeness to the name of any person, living or dead, is purely coincidental.

Scripture quotations from The Authorized (King James) Version. Rights in the Authorized Version in the United Kingdom are vested in the Crown. Reproduced by permission of the Crown's patentee, Cambridge University Press.

CHAPTER 1

"You are one of two. You were a perfect pair, but your mother could only keep one of you. She kept the other twin."

Those words burned into Emma's memory like a branding iron. She knew from that moment onward she had been abandoned.

Emma opened her eyes and still saw the image of her grandmother's lips forming each word—the same lips that never uttered another sound about Emma's mother or twin sister. Whenever Emma prodded for more information it was quickly silenced.

There was one day when Emma was around nine that she was determined to get some answers.

Her grandmother sat on the front porch, her feet crossed at the ankles, and a cup of tea in her right hand. Emma was on an old chair next to her, playing with the frayed strings of her apron, waiting for her grandmother to answer her question about where her mother was. Emma waited for what seemed like minutes, and then her grandmother finally replied. She told her she was too young to know right now.

The whispered words from long ago were the only evidence Emma had from her grandmother.

From then on, the only way Emma obtained information about her family was by way of overheard gossip from the community's members. She learned her grandmother's words had reflected exactly what had happened.

It was scandalous and Emma wondered how a mother could split up the bond of twins. What kind of person could do that?

Today was Emma's eighteenth birthday, and she was already looking to the future. She knew that if she wanted anything different in life, she'd have to take some risks and do something about it.

She was determined to break away from life's monotony and seek out something new and thrilling—a quest to find her twin.

That was what she wanted more than anything else.

She sat up and looked around the room, which hadn't changed in years. Most likely, it was like this when she'd been abandoned there as a baby.

The room was still plain, with a lamp in the corner to light up the dark nights and a rocking chair in the center facing the bed. No one ever sat in that rocking chair. A mother was supposed to sit and rock their child, but it had never happened. A large picture window overlooked a small field with a red barn in the distance.

Emma's gaze was drawn upward, up to the single gaslight that hung from a chain. She'd stare at that light for hours, lost in thought, wondering about the twin she never knew.

No matter how hard she tried, she couldn't shake the feeling of being incomplete.

She would often stare at her reflection, imagining what her sister would look like. Would she share Emma's blue eyes and strawberry blonde curls, or would she look completely different?

She'd heard stories about twin bonds which led her to wonder if her twin missed her too.

As was the natural state of things, growing up without siblings caused Emma to be the odd one out in the small community. All her friends had so many brothers and sisters. Emma only had her grandmother; her grandfather had died years before she was born.

Emma's birthday meant she had no chores, and what's more, *Mammi* would cook all her favorite food. Her grandmother had told her she'd invited five friends to dinner, and Emma desperately hoped that one would be Hosea. Emma was sure that every girl in the county was in love with the handsome Hosea, and she would do everything to ensure that she would be his wife.

Emma lay in bed daydreaming about Hosea. She imagined him sweeping her off her feet and taking her away from this small town—somewhere they could live a life of excitement.

Emma stretched her hands over her head, threw back her quilt and sat up. Then she got out of bed. Pulling aside the curtains, she peeped out her bedroom window at the cornfield and the charming red barn in the distance. Her grandmother's house was surrounded by fields and forests.

It was a peaceful place, but Emma needed something different. She needed adventure, passion, and love. Although, she would miss that view if she ever left this house.

The sun was nearing the top of the sky, which meant it was mid-morning—a good time to get out of bed for a birthday girl.

If it were just a normal day, she would have been up at the crack of dawn to do chores such as gardening, cooking, or cleaning. Her grandmother kept a tight schedule, and every day was filled with all manner of chores. The exceptions were Sundays and, of course, birthdays.

Emma sighed. How she longed for a part-time job like some of the other girls in the community, but her grandmother insisted she wait until she was a little older. She hoped that eighteen was old enough. Her grandmother didn't specify an age.

Emma changed into her best dress, placed her prayer *kapp* carefully on her head, and went downstairs. She knew from the silence that her grandmother was out, most likely at the markets picking up goodies for her birthday dinner.

As Emma made herself breakfast, she heard a car outside. She ignored it, assuming it to be tourists who had lost their way. Tourists in Lancaster County were always curious about their Amish lifestyle and often drove by with cameras or phones out the window taking pictures.

When a loud knock on the door rang through Emma's ears, she knew it was no tourist – they never knocked.

Emma threw down her spoon and rushed to the door.

Emma's mouth fell to the ground when she flung the door open and saw a young woman.

It was as if she was looking in a mirror.

It had to be her twin. There was no one else it could be. This was the special twin, the one her mother had chosen to keep.

CHAPTER 2

"Happy Birthday to you," her twin said with a huge smile.

Emma gasped and held her stomach as she gazed at the stranger, who wasn't really a stranger. Even her voice was like her own. She started at the top of her head, and her gaze traveled down to her feet. Her twin was dressed in English clothing—jeans and a blouse, with a leather jacket slung over her shoulder.

Everything about her twin gave the impression she didn't have a care in the world. Her twin's eyes were perhaps a darker shade of blue, or maybe the lighting made them so.

"Hello," Emma stammered, unsure of what to say. "I didn't know I had a twin. I did, but I don't think I am supposed to know. No one told me anything, not directly. You are my twin, aren't you?"

"Undoubtedly. I know what you mean. It's been the

same for me. You were never mentioned." Her twin stepped into the house. "I've been searching for you for years. They've been keeping you under wraps, but I found you."

Emma stepped back in shock as her twin dropped her bag just inside the door, dropped her coat on top, and walked past her into the kitchen. She followed her and then watched in silence as her twin poured herself a glass of water and then took a seat at the table.

"You don't seem too surprised." Emma's twin looked over at her.

"I am," Emma replied, still in shock. "I just don't know what to say."

"I understand,"

"I'm so happy you're here, though. I've always wanted to meet you. It's been a dream of mine."

"Me too. I'm Isobel, by the way."

"I'm Emma."

"I know."

"Oh."

"Is there anyone else here?" Isobel looked over Emma's shoulder.

"No. My grandmother will probably be out for a while. Can I hug you?"

"Sure." Isobel stood up.

Emma wrapped her arms around her sister. She'd waited for this day her whole life. The two girls hugged right there in their grandmother's kitchen. It was something she never thought would happen, not here and not like this. Emma breathed in Isobel's perfume which was sweet and flowery.

Emma stepped back, breaking their embrace. "Is our mother here too?" Emma hurried to the window, hoping to see her mother. The car had gone.

"No. I came alone."

"Where's your car?"

"That was an Uber."

"Oh."

Isobel looked Emma up and down and murmured something that Emma couldn't make out.

"What was that?"

Isobel smiled at Emma. "I haven't seen you before, not in my living memory. It feels like I've found a part of myself," Isobel said.

"Me too. I don't know why we were separated. I've longed for this day. I can't wait for *Mammi* to meet you. Are you staying with us? Oh, please say yes."

"Wait, what? No! And you can't tell anyone I'm here." Isobel drank the rest of the water and then set the glass down.

"Why? I've got people coming for my birthday, and this is the best thing I could ever have prayed for. I've so many questions for you, and I'm sure you've got so much to ask me. Wait, it's your birthday too. We'll have a combined birthday celebration."

"People are coming here? When?"

"Later today."

"I don't get excited about birthdays and all that."

"I don't even know your last name; is it the same as mine?"

"Tell me what yours is then, and I'll tell you."

"Byler."

Isobel gave a little laugh. "So's mine. No great surprise there."

Emma noticed that tears started to spill down Isobel's face. She'd gone from happy and smiling to tears in less than five seconds. "Isobel, whatever is the matter?"

"My boyfriend," is all Isobel said.

"Is he all right?"

Isobel nodded. "Unfortunately, he is. He dumped me."

Emma had never heard that expression before, but she knew what it meant by the way Isobel was sobbing. "I'm so sorry."

Through tears, Isobel looked at Emma. "Where's your room?"

"Upstairs. Come with me. I'll take your bag."

Isobel quietly followed Emma up the creaky, wooden stairs to Emma's room. Once they were in the bedroom, Isobel sat heavily on Emma's bed. "Emma, I don't have much time. I have an idea, and I hope you'll agree."

"First, I've got so much to ask you. Where's our mother, and where do you live? Do you live close by?" Emma wanted to ask, *why did my mother keep you and not me?* She knew she could not blurt something like that out, not when they'd just met. That was a question for another time. Eventually, that would have to be answered. Maybe she would have to wait and find out from her mother directly.

Isobel said, "Later, don't worry about that now."

"Is our mother okay? She isn't sick or anything, is she?" Emma was terrified that her long-lost mother would die before they ever got to meet.

Isobel shrugged. "Still the same old mom," she said.

Hearing those words made Emma feel a wave of relief pass through her body. She had no idea what her mother looked and sounded like; in her mind, she was still a stranger. Even if their mother appeared at the door, Emma wouldn't recognize her.

Knowing Isobel wasn't responsible for their mother's decision from eighteen years ago, Emma tried to push away the envy rising inside her. Nonetheless, it was the painful truth—Emma was always going to be the unwanted twin.

CHAPTER 3

"This room is so dull and boring," Isobel said, turning around in a full circle. "And so small."

"The quilt's bright." Emma sat down and ran her hand over the quilt. *"Mammi* made it before I was born."

"It's old. Time to get a new one."

Emma opened her mouth in shock. Get a new one? The quilt was an heirloom that Emma would pass down to her children.

Isobel turned a little so she could face Emma squarely, and then she said, "So, as I said, I have things to ask you."

"Sure. Ask me anything and then I've got so many questions for you."

Isobel leaned forward, looking Emma straight in the eyes. "I need your help. You see, I've gotten myself into a bit of a situation." She paused, biting her lip. "I need a place to lay low for a few days. Just until things cool down."

"What kind of situation?" Emma asked.

"I can't face going back to my life. I need a break."

Emma's heart raced at seeing her twin so upset. "How can I help?"

Isobel's eyes lit up. "You're the only one I trust, Emma. I know I can count on you." She reached out and grabbed Emma's hand.

Emma looked down at their hands, and a rush of emotion filled her heart. They were identical, which meant they started from one cell. They were the same.

"I think we should trade places."

Emma looked up. "What do you mean?"

Isobel continued, "You be me, and I'll be you. We look the same, and no one will ever know."

Emma remained silent, and Isobel let go of her hand.

Isobel ignored Emma's silence and continued, "I'm in college, but I can't go back there. Not now that Travis has dumped me. I can't face all those people. I just need a rest for a week or so."

Emma sighed and laid a hand on Isobel's shoulder. "You can stay here and rest for as long as you like. My grandmother never talks about you, but she'd love you as much as she loves me. How could she not?"

"It's like this, Emma. I need someone to be me for a while, and who is better than you? It's a perfect arrangement for both of us. I've thought it all through. You can see our mother. Surely, you'd want to meet her, right?"

"Oh yes."

"She visits me every now and again. Just don't tell her that we've swapped places." Isobel bounced on the bed.

"I can't. I don't want to meet her in that way. And I also know nothing of the *English* world, well, hardly anything."

"It's easy to learn. I've made up a plan." Isobel swallowed hard and then took a deep breath. "I brought you a phone, and you can call me and ask me anything you need to. You can even text me, and I can text you back." Isobel reached over and pulled two cell phones from her oversized bag.

Emma's eyes widened at the phone. It hadn't occurred to her that Isobel would use a phone, but of course, Isobel would know all about them.

Why had Isobel assumed she'd agree to her crazy plan? She must've thought she'd do it or she wouldn't be offering her a phone. "It'll never work, Isobel. Our only telephone is in the barn, and we hardly ever use it. It's a dial-up phone where you put your finger in the number and turn it. I don't know how to use a cell."

"It's easy. This is my phone, and this is the one I got for you. I'll show you how to use it. It's simple. There's nothing to it. Even a child can use a phone, and you're smarter than a little kid, aren't you?" She passed Emma the phone.

The phone was small and sleek and fit nicely into Emma's hand. She felt intimidated just holding it. "I can't do it. No, I just can't. Someone will find out, and I'll get into trouble. Besides, I don't know you, so I don't know how to be you." Emma licked her lips. She wanted to please her twin, but it was plain to see Isobel wouldn't be happy unless Emma agreed with the plan. "Why is it so important?"

"I need this. Just listen first. If you attend my lessons, that's all you'll have to do. You won't have to talk with anyone. I've got someone sending things to me by email. I'll do all the assignments and essays. See? No problem." Isobel flicked her long hair away from her face. " It'll just be for six months. You'll live in my apartment and go to my classes on campus. And keep to yourself. How simple could that be? Simple, right? Please say yes, Emma. And after that, we can be together and really get to know each other."

Emma loved the idea of getting to know Isobel. "You want to spend time with me?"

"More than anything else in the world. You're my twin. You're part of me. Please do this one thing for me. I'll never ask for anything again."

Emma sucked in her bottom lip. "Six months? I can't do that. I'm sorry." Then Emma considered it for a while. Her grandmother would not even allow her to get a part-time job, so who knows when she would be able to see what the *outside* world was like? She had been yearning for excitement. "I guess I could do it, but just for a week like you said at first." Emma shook her head quickly. "No, this is madness. I don't know where you live. How would I get there?"

"I've got all that covered. I've worked it all out." Isobel

leaned over, reached into her bag, and produced a thick notebook. "Here are all the instructions. There are maps, directions to transport, pictures of my friends, and information about them." Isobel gave the book to Emma. "It's all there – my life."

Emma flipped through the pages of the heavy book. This was delightful. Now she had a way to know all about Isobel and her life.

"Don't look at it now. You'll have plenty of time to read it on the bus back home."

Emma's head jerked up. "Bus? Back home?"

"New York, where I live – well, where you'll live – for the next... little while."

Emma swallowed hard. Was this the opportunity for which she'd been waiting? She did want to get to know Isobel, and maybe this was the perfect way for them to find out about each other's lives. "You said you don't live with our mother?"

"No, she lives with her boyfriend, Frank, about an hour's drive away. I live – well, you will live by yourself in my small apartment. It's not great or big, but at least it's home." Isobel took two credit cards from her bag and handed them to Emma. "This one you can get cash out with, and this one you can pay for things with. Frank has a lot of money, so spend up." Isobel giggled. "Well, not too much, or mom will call you and yell at you, but you can get everything you need. Frank pays for the rent on the apartment, so you don't have to worry about that. Use all my stuff. I've got loads of clothes. Wear anything you want."

Emma ran her finger over the raised name on the cards and said the name. "Frank Guido. So, you live on Frank's money?"

Isobel nodded. "Have ever since mom's been with him, which is a few years now."

"He sounds like a very nice man to look after you and our mother so well."

Isobel shook her head. "I tolerate him. He has a lot of money."

"You don't like him?" Emma raised her eyebrows and studied her twin's face.

"He's okay, I suppose. Better than a lot of the other boyfriends she's had."

Emma wished she could remember something of her mother, a smell, a sound, but she recalled nothing. "What became of our father? Do you know him?"

Isobel shrugged her shoulders. "No. Who knows where he is – who cares?"

Both girls turned their heads to the sound of a clip-clopping outside the house.

"That'll be our grandmother," Emma said.

Isobel pulled on Emma's arm. "She can't know about this."

Emma looked down at her arm that Isobel was clutching tightly. "Ow, you're hurting me. I haven't agreed to anything."

"You did. You just said that you would, didn't you?" Isobel held her arm tighter.

Emma freed herself from Isobel's grasp. "If I did, it wasn't a definite yes. My brain is in shock. I need to think about this. Can't I just ask *Mammi* if it's okay? It won't matter if she knows. She won't tell anyone. I guess she might try to stop me, but I'll tell her I'm eighteen and can do what I want."

Isobel's eyes became red, and then tears started to well up and spill down her cheeks.

"Don't cry, Isobel." Emma rushed to put an arm around her.

Between sobs, Isobel said, "It won't work if we tell anyone. She'll try to stop you, and you won't do it. I was hoping that you would just do this one thing for me. It's not hard, and I've spent a lot of time planning it." Through tear-filled eyes, Isobel continued, "I've always wanted to be with you and do things with you, and now you won't do this one thing I've asked you."

Emma inhaled deeply. "It's a huge thing, though, Isobel." When Isobel continued to cry, Emma hugged her a little tighter. "How would you live my life? Do you even know anything about our ways?"

"I've read a lot about the Amish, and mom even used to speak Pennsylvania Dutch to me when I was younger. I think I remember a lot of it, so yeah, I can do it."

"Really? Our mother spoke Pennsylvania Dutch to you?"

Isobel nodded. "And I know some German too. See? I'm prepared to be you."

"We have a different accent."

"We'll have to change the way we talk, okay? Simple. Pretend you're an actor playing a part."

Emma took her arm away from Isobel and looked out the window. "It'll take *Mammi* a little while to unhitch the buggy and tend to the horse."

"Emma, I was certain you would do this for me. I've gone through a lot of trouble organizing this. Can you do it for me, please, as your twin sister? This is the only thing I will ever ask of you… ever."

"I'm scared." Emma sat on the bed. "What if it doesn't work, and we get into a whole heap of trouble?"

Isobel shrugged. "If it doesn't work, it doesn't work. So, who cares?" She leaned close to Emma. "But it will work."

Emma remembered again how she longed to take a look at the *English* world and how her grandmother was so strict. The only thing she would miss about her life, besides *Mammi*, would be Hosea. But Hosea wasn't going anywhere. He'd still be there when she got back.

Emma looked into Isobel's eyes. "I'll do it if it's just for a week."

Isobel jumped up and down. "You will?"

Emma nodded, and suddenly a wave of nausea hit her stomach. Emma had tried lying once when she was younger and found that she was not good at it; since then, she had always tried to be truthful. Now she would be deceiving people without even opening her mouth. Still, she would be learning about her twin and her mother, and that was worth the risk. The smile on Isobel's face confirmed she was making the right choice.

"The bus leaves at one this afternoon." Isobel looked at her watch.

"What today?" Emma's hand flew to her mouth as it opened in shock.

"Yes." Isobel held up her bag. "I have clothes in here for you. Call a taxi and have it collect you a little way up the road so your grandmother won't see."

"Our grandmother," Emma corrected her.

"Our grandmother." Isobel nodded. "You call her *Mammi?"*

"That's right."

"That's easy enough to remember."

Emma steeled herself for the answer to the question she was about to ask. "Where am I going?"

"The address is in your guidebook. Well, first you're going to the bus station. Then the bus will take you to a New York terminal. Get a taxi when you get off the bus and give the driver the address written in your book. It's easy." Isobel grabbed the notebook, opened the first page, and tapped a finger heavily on the address. "I've thought of everything. I'm a good planner."

Emma swallowed hard and wished that she had not agreed to Isobel's bold plan. It was too hard to say 'no' to her twin. "So, I guess I have to leave, like right now or very soon?"

"Yes, isn't it exciting? I knew you'd agree because

we're twins, so we're alike. I'm spontaneous, and so are you."

"I guess. I have been wanting some excitement in my life."

"See? We're the same. We're two halves of a whole."

"I wish we could spend more time together, Isobel."

"Yes. We will. We can do that later, I promise."

Emma nodded. "Okay. I'll do it."

"Good. You'll have to put makeup on and wear my clothes." Isobel tipped the contents of the backpack over the bed and proceeded to pass Emma some *Englisch* clothes.

"I know how to put makeup on. A friend of mine used to sneak her older sister's makeup, and we'd put it on. Her sister was hiding the makeup, so when she found out Betty was sneaking it, she couldn't tell her *mamm*." Emma gave a little giggle.

Isobel just stared at Emma with an expressionless face.

Noticing Isobel's demeanor, Emma explained, "We can't wear makeup, didn't you know?"

"Yes, I know that, but I was just wondering about the rest of the jabber you were going on with." Isobel shook her head. "Quick, what things do you need to tell me?"

Emma held her head. "No. I can't do this."

"Live a little, Emma. You just said you long for excitement in your life."

Emma stared at her twin. "I'm scared about leaving

home. I've never really gone anywhere, but I want to. I just don't know if the timing is right."

"Don't think about it so much. Take a leap of faith. It'll be fun. Spread your wings and fly like a bird. If things go bad, just come back."

Emma slowly nodded.

"You have nothing to lose, do you?" Isobel asked.

"Nothing at all."

"Great."

"Don't forget I'm having a birthday party tonight. *Mammi* has invited some of my friends, and there's this one boy I like, Hosea. I'm hoping she's invited him." Emma's face fell. "Now I won't be here to see him, and I'll miss my special meal too."

"What?" Isobel screwed up her face. "You don't know who she's invited?"

Emma shook her head.

"So, you call him a boy? Why don't you call him a man?"

"I don't know. He is a young man. I'm not sure why I call him a boy."

"That's ridiculous that you don't get a say about who's invited to your own birthday party. You're treated as a child." Isobel made gagging sounds as she clutched at her throat. "They're strangling you, Emma, and you don't even know it. I've come at just the right time."

"I'm not treated like a child. I just have to respect people who are older and in authority."

Isobel raised her eyebrows. "No one's going to treat

me like that," she murmured to herself. "I can see I'm gonna have to make some changes around here."

Emma zipped up the jeans and then grabbed the T-shirt. "It is only for a week, isn't it?"

"That's right, Emma. It's just for a week. No problem there." Isobel took off her wristwatch and fastened it to Emma's wrist.

CHAPTER 4

"Quickly, what are some other things I should know?" Isobel asked.

"The first thing you should know is that there are chores, loads of them."

"Oh great." Isobel rolled her eyes. "Any special things about the chores that I'll need to know?"

"Well, for cooking, you can always follow the recipe cards. They're from our great-grandmother, and they're kept in the bottom drawer opposite the stove."

Isobel gave a nod. "Got it. What else? Hurry, Emma, you're speaking too slowly."

Emma tilted her chin upward. "That's how I normally speak. I notice that you speak very quickly."

Isobel rolled her eyes once more. "Okay, I'll have to remember that too; talk slowly. You'll have to talk faster. Now, what else?"

"*Mammi* keeps a list of my weekly chores, and it's kept in the same drawer as the recipes."

"Sounds a bit controlling, but okay—a list of chores in the recipe drawer. What about your friends? What do I need to know about them?" Isobel took a notebook and pen from her bag. "Tell me their names."

"My best friend is Mary Miller, and there's Katie Lapp and Lizzy Lapp. Lizzy and Katie are sisters. Then there's Hosea, who I've already mentioned, and then there's David King."

As Isobel finished writing their names, she asked, "Now, quickly tell me a little about each one."

"Well, Hosea …"

Isobel cut across Emma's words. "Yeah, you're in love with him, I remember. Who's next?"

Emma pursed her lips together at her twin's rudeness but carried on regardless. "The next one I'll tell you about is David King. He lives next door and is a nice boy and a very good singer. He sings at just about every singing we go to. He's tall and very skinny with dark hair."

Isobel was still writing as she said, "Ah, singings. I've read about them on the internet. There's just singing, isn't there, and no music?"

"*Jah*." Emma nodded.

"What about harmonizing?"

Emma tipped her head to the side. "What's that?"

Isobel shook her head. "Forget it. Come on, keep telling me about your friends."

"Then there's Katie and Lizzy. Lizzy is one year older.

They're both close friends of mine. Lizzy works at the flower market, and Katie works at a pizza place."

Isobel glanced up at her sister. "You don't look very happy about that."

"It's just that I want a job too, even a part-time one, but *Mammi* won't let me until I'm older."

Isobel shook her head. "I'll work on getting her to let you have a job."

"Would you?"

"Yes, but I don't want to do the job, you'll have to come back before I have to start."

Emma giggled. "Thanks, Isobel. I'll do any kind of job at all."

"I'll make sure it's a good job. What else?" Isobel asked, hurrying her along.

"I think I've left someone out." Emma looked up at the ceiling. "Oh yes, then there's my very best friend in the world, and that's Mary. We went to school together and we tell each other all our secrets." Emma pushed out her bottom lip and then said in a low voice, "That is, we used to tell all our secrets until we both started to like Hosea."

Isobel laughed. "I can't wait to meet this Hosea. He must be quite something."

Emma drew her hands to her heart, and her face lit up. "Oh, he is. I want to marry him someday. I will one day, I'm sure of it."

"Well, I shall have to keep an eye on him when you're gone."

"You'd do that for me, Isobel?"

"Sure, what are sisters for? Especially twin sisters – that's even more special. We're like two halves," Isobel said.

Emma rushed to Isobel and hugged her as she remembered the words her grandmother uttered years before about being two halves of a whole. "I've wanted us to be together since we were parted. I've felt you were missing. I felt it deep inside. I wish I didn't have to go away; there are so many things I want to tell you and ask you."

"We can do all that later – I promise." Isobel hugged her sister tightly and then pushed her away. "We haven't got a lot of time. I've given you the cell phone, and I've written down everything I can think of."

"I'm still scared. What if I don't know something? What if I can't speak with you for some reason?" Emma nibbled the end of a fingernail.

"If it's just general information on things, you could 'Google it.'"

"Google?"

"On the Internet. Oh, you don't know about computers, do you?"

"I know a little bit. Mary and I went to the library and had a lesson on computers, so I know a little."

"Google is a search engine, which means you can ask the computer anything you want to know. It's quite surprising the things it will bring up. I learned a little of the Amish ways before I came here, and of course, Mom's always told me stories of the Amish." Isobel gave a little shrug.

"I think I'll be able to do that. Do you have a computer?" Emma heard her own voice shaking a little.

"Yes, I brought a small laptop with me, and I have a laptop computer in my apartment you can use; it's in the bedroom."

"I hope I don't make a mess of anything for you." Emma wondered if she could really go through with this, and if she did, could they both really pull it off without anyone realizing it?

"No, you couldn't possibly mess anything up. Just pretend to be me and sit through my lessons. You can even pretend to take notes. It's a piece of cake, trust me. If someone thinks you're not yourself, just pretend that you hit your head or you feel sick or something along those lines."

Emma looked into Isobel's face. "You do look exactly the same as I do. I hope that's enough."

Isobel put her arms out toward Emma, and Emma stepped in and hugged her. "Dear sweet innocent, Emma." Isobel patted Emma lightly on her back.

A chill ran through Emma's body as her sister spoke those words. It was as if she were going to steal her life or something of the sort. *Nee, I'm just nervous about going away from home. That's all it is,* she reasoned.

Isobel abruptly pushed Emma away. "Now I have to change my clothes." She glanced at the clothes hanging up. "I suppose I'll have to wear that every day, won't I?"

Emma looked at her clothes. *"Jah,* of course. I have four dresses, each one a different color."

"Wow, four dresses. What an extravagant life you lead."

"You up there, Emma?" Her grandmother's voice rang from downstairs.

Emma's heart immediately raced as guilt coursed through her body. *"Jah, Mammi,* I'll be down in a minute."

"Nee, stay up there if you wish. It's your birthday, so you can do whatever you want today."

"Okay, *Mammi,* I'll be down later, if that's okay," Emma said.

Her grandmother did not reply.

Isobel flipped open her cell phone and arranged for an Uber to wait for Emma at the end of the road.

CHAPTER 5

From the small window in Emma's bedroom, Isobel watched Emma scurrying up the street, dressed as herself. She laughed and threw herself onto Emma's bed. Now she could have the rest she needed, away from the drama of college life and away from people who say they are her friends and then talk about her behind her back. Most of all, she would be away from Travis, the man who broke her heart. "Yes, this will be my perfect vacation – in Amish land."

"You still up there, Emma?"

Isobel could only hope her voice was similar to Emma's; otherwise, her holiday would only last a day. "I'm still up here in the bedroom, *Mammi*."

"Ahh, very well," her grandmother replied.

Isobel stayed on the bed, a little nervous about venturing out of the bedroom. How she wished she had asked Emma just a few more questions. She put her phone on silent and hid it under the pillow, then turned her attention to Emma's clothes.

She chose a plum-colored dress, which she thought to be the prettiest. She covered the dress with an apron and pulled on Emma's thick stockings. Isobel walked over to the large bowl used as a washbasin and picked up the folded washcloth beside it. Once Isobel had wrung out the excess water, she proceeded to scrub off her makeup.

She looked for a mirror but remembered that a lot of Amish folks shunned mirrors so they didn't become vain. "Ridiculous idea," she said under her breath.

How on earth am I supposed to see how I look? I hope my mascara hasn't run under my eyes.

Isobel used the window where she was able to see a dim reflection.

Once she was satisfied that she had removed all her makeup, she wound her thick, wavy hair up on top of her head, pinned it, then placed the white prayer *kapp* on her head.

I can't believe that people wear this every single day. What a bother.

Isobel intended to creep down the stairs unnoticed, but due to the creaking sounds that came with each step, it was impossible. When she reached the bottom, she came face to face with her grandmother, who was dusting the living room.

"Finally, out of bed, I see. Remember, it's only today

you don't have chores. Tomorrow it's back to normal." When the old lady smiled at her, Isobel noticed she had kind eyes.

"*Jah.*" Isobel smiled back at her grandmother, whom she was meeting for the first time. Her grandmother was small and plump, nothing like her mom, who was tall and slender.

"Your new dress looks nice."

Isobel looked down at her dress. "*Denke.*"

The older woman went back to dusting, and when Isobel was nearly at the front door, *Mammi* asked, "Did you fix yourself some food while I was out?"

Isobel was not hungry at all because excitement was gnawing away at her stomach. The last thing she wanted was food. "*Jah,* I did, *denke.*"

"Good."

Isobel had fooled her grandmother all the way from the foot of the stairs to the front door. As she opened the door, Isobel said, "I'll just go take a walk for a little while."

"Fine. Dinner will be at the usual time, and I've got your friends coming a little before that. Don't be late."

Isobel nodded as she walked through the door. "*Jah,* I'll watch the time."

"You know how you get to daydreaming and forget everything."

"Okay." Isobel closed the door behind her and stepped into the warm sunshine. She welcomed the cool breeze that caressed her face.

As she walked into the field, she wondered how Emma, or any Amish woman for that matter, tolerated the heavy dress, the apron, and the bothersome prayer *kapp*. She was unhappy that she would have to wear the outfit every day for six months.

It wasn't going to be just a week like she'd told Emma. No! She'd find a way to prolong Emma's stay. She'd had to bend the truth a little to make Emma do the swap.

A little further into Isobel's walk, she forgot all about the aggravation of her heavy, unflattering clothing. Clean air was filling her lungs, and she was loving the peace and quiet.

She turned and looked back at the large farmhouse, which now looked tiny. Would her mom have grown up in that very house? She had often wondered why her mom never visited her twin and had never gone back to fetch her when she became financially stable.

A smile spread over Isobel's face at how clever she'd been to keep the Lancaster County address she had seen on a letter that arrived at her mother's house years before. Something had told Isobel to get that envelope out of the trash and keep it. She knew that letter had to be from the grandmother she had never met.

Isobel turned her back on the old farmhouse and continued her walk. As she looked down at Emma's black boots, she wondered how Emma was getting along. She hoped that she hadn't thrown her twin to the wolves. Isobel chose not to worry about Emma; she needed to worry about herself and how she was going to fool people into thinking that she was Emma, a truly innocent and simple Amish girl. That would be quite a performance, but she was more than ready for her opening scene.

CHAPTER 6

*E*mma got out of the Uber and then wandered around the crowded bus station until she came across the ticket window. She purchased a one-way ticket to New York with Isobel's plastic card. The woman she bought the ticket from looked bored.

Emma considered that maybe that woman had come to the same job for the last thirty years. She too would have that same look on her face if she were forced to do the same thing over and over. That made Emma glad that she was doing something out of the ordinary. At least she wasn't having a dull life, as the lady at the ticket window appeared to have.

Emma turned from the window and placed the ticket carefully in Isobel's purse. Her attention was then taken by several screens high on the wall with the bus times flashing on them. Emma walked over to see if she could see exactly where her bus would leave. In half an hour, she was to go out door number two and hopefully find her bus.

She took a seat with the crowds of waiting people and was suddenly conscious of the ripped jeans she was wearing. Emma could see the pale skin of her legs through the holes. With her legs covered by heavy stockings every day, they had never seen the sun.

Emma pressed back into the uncomfortable plastic seat. She would never have thought she would be dressed in clothes such as these. As soon as she got to Isobel's apartment, she would find more suitable clothes.

Emma's thick hair was caught up behind her head in a band instead of hiding in her usual prayer *kapp*. Emma was self-conscious about being out in public without her prayer *kapp* for the first time since she was a little girl. She could not help but wonder whether what she was doing was a sin in *Gott's* eyes.

Had she been too eager to please the twin she was separated from for eighteen years? Maybe if she'd had a little more time to think about it, she would have found the courage to say 'no' to Isobel.

Emma's heart pumped wildly. She was finally going to see what the *English* world was like; she also had a chance to be independent without *Mammi,* or anyone else, watching over her. She looked around about her again. No one was looking at her or had even noticed her; she had complete freedom.

Emma had never desired to live the *Englisch* lifestyle as some of her acquaintances had done on their *rumspringa,* but she did want to know what it was like and had figured she'd have to do that from the sidelines.

Emma's only regret was that she would not be able to see Hosea for a whole week. She was sure her grandmother would have invited him to her birthday dinner because she'd dropped enough hints. Emma's grandmother and Hosea's grandmother were best friends. Emma hoped they would put their heads together one day and do a little matchmaking for Hosea and herself.

As she sat on the uncomfortable seat at the bus station, she opened Isobel's life manual and read from the first page. She hoped she would learn something about her mother.

Before she had finished the first two pages, an announcement came over the loudspeaker that the bus to New York was boarding. Emma gathered her belongings and climbed aboard, ready for the adventure of her life.

CHAPTER 7

Hours later, Isobel was still in the fields. She was in the middle of nowhere, which was just what she needed. Recalling her grandmother's warning about being late, she considered it best to start walking back.

Knowing that she was bad with directions, Isobel had made sure she had walked in a perfectly straight line. Now all she had to do was turn around and walk back the same way.

"Emma, wait."

Isobel heard a man's voice and looked around to see an Amish man hurrying toward her. She stopped and waited.

As he drew closer, she knew in her heart that he had to be Hosea. Her heart melted when she saw the warm smile on his face. His hair was dark brown and wavy, and his eyes were the bluest of blue, complimented by his sun-kissed skin.

As soon as he caught up, he gave her a dazzling smile.

"Happy birthday, Emma."

"*Denke*, and are you coming to my party?" This man was just as good-looking as Travis, maybe even more so. His hair was longish, like most Amish men, but his face had strength and kindness about it that she'd never seen in a face before.

"Indeed, I am."

His voice was melodious and thrilling to her ears. She couldn't help thinking that Emma was a fool to leave him. "What have you been doing today?"

"I've been working in the fields, like I do most days." His attitude was relaxed, and he had a peaceful, assured demeanor that Isobel found attractive.

She glanced at his arms, which, even beneath his oversized Amish garments displayed an impressive muscularity.

"And what about you?" His hands rested on his hips as he questioned her.

"I had a marvelous day off from chores, strolling in the sunshine and taking in *Gott's* fresh air." She figured Emma would say something like that. Isobel noticed Hosea was looking at her intently as she spoke.

"You seem different today, Emma. What have you done?"

"Yes, I'm eighteen now. A grown woman!" Isobel giggled, knowing Hosea had no idea she had traded places with her twin sister. It seemed none of the people in their community were even aware that Emma had a twin.

"Ah, that must be it then." Hosea smiled.

"Did you bring me a present, Hosea?"

Hosea chuckled. "Your grandmother said not to bother with gifts."

Isobel stepped closer, admiring his rugged beauty. She inhaled deeply and caught the scent of earthy rain mixed with wood smoke. "How about a kiss instead?"

He grinned at her request. "I love this playful side of you. You're usually so serious." Hosea lifted his hand and playfully covered Isobel's face for a moment.

The smell of lavender and field grasses filled Isobel's nose, and she playfully pushed his hand away and laughed along with him, although she had been serious about the kiss request. His heart was genuine, and she knew he would not do what Travis had done. She pondered that if all Amish men were as kind-hearted as Hosea she could get used to living an Amish life for a while.

Hosea grabbed her hand and directed her gaze toward the sky. "Emma, what does that cloud look like?"

"A horse's head," she replied without hesitation.

"Do you remember when we used to lie on the grass and find shapes in the clouds when we were kids?"

"Yes! Let's do it now!" Excitedly, Isobel lay down on the grass with him following close behind. The grass was sharp on her legs as the blades pushed through her black stockings, but she didn't care.

He pointed out another formation in the sky. "What about this one? What does it look like to you?"

Isobel's gaze followed where he pointed. "That one is…

just a cloud, I think. Hey look at that. The clouds are going in two different directions."

"It's just the air currents I'd say. One is going one way and the other is going the opposite. I haven't seen that before," Hosea said.

"Me neither." Isobel stared at the clouds, and it popped into her mind that they were just like herself and Emma traveling along different paths.

"C'mon, Emma. Your grandmother is going to be angry if we keep you from your birthday plans. Let's go!" Hosea stood up and put out his hand for Isobel. She grabbed his hand, and he pulled her to her feet. His hand was rough and warm, giving her an odd feeling of comfort and security.

"Wait," she said. "I'm not ready to be done yet. You have to tell me what two more clouds look like first. Then we can go."

"Okay," he said with a laugh. "But only because it's your birthday." He lay back down in the grass and pointed. "That one looks like a haystack with a pitchfork sticking out of it. Oh, and that one? That one should be easy: it's a tree. Couldn't you see that for yourself?" He poked her in the ribs.

"Ow! Stop that, Hosea," she joked. Isobel went to give him a playful slap, but he rolled out of her way and then jumped to his feet.

She followed suit, but he was now running away from her. She went after him. He dodged her outstretched hands a few times until they both ended up falling on the ground laughing together.

After their laughter died down, they looked into each other's eyes until Hosea said with a smile, "C'mon now, or else I'll get you that present you wanted, and we'll both be in trouble." He reached his hand out toward her, and she took it firmly as he pulled her to her feet once again.

As they headed back to Emma's house, Isobel found herself almost running to keep up with Hosea's lengthy strides. She cast him an admiring glance. She had to make this man her boyfriend while she was here.

"What were you looking at there, Emma Byler?"

Isobel wanted to tell him my future husband, but instead she just laughed and said "Nothing."

Hosea dropped his gaze to the ground, shaking his head. "You are a grown woman now at eighteen, Emma. Your laugh today made me think of our younger days. We had so much fun, you and I."

"Yes, we did have lots of fun," she replied softly, wondering if something serious was coming next.

"Would you allow me to give you a ride home after the next singing?"

Isobel stopped walking and Hosea stopped as well. "Yes, I would like that a lot, Hosea." She knew from her research about the Amish ways and customs that this would be an official date.

"Me too," he said before continuing forward. "Let's keep moving. You know how strict your grandmother is about time! If we're late, she won't stop going on about it."

"That's true," Isobel agreed while taking in—again—how strong and good-looking he was. She pondered once more why Emma had agreed to leave.

CHAPTER 8

On the bus, Emma became bored with looking at Isobel's notebook, so she switched her gaze to outside the window. She was fortunate enough to have a window seat and no one next to her. Surprisingly, she felt a sense of peace rather than anxiety. It could've been because she would soon find out the secrets of her past.

Emma took out the box the cell phone had come in and started reading the instructions. She quickly noticed that it needed electricity to be charged. Had Isobel considered this? Where did she plan on charging it?

Emma's heart sank as the reality of Isobel's situation began to dawn on her. Without any way to recharge her phone, Isobel would be unable to ask Emma questions when she needed help.

When everyone had gotten off the bus, Emma stepped out and saw people running around in all directions. All the commotion was daunting. She followed a stream of people heading toward the city bus, then she hopped into a taxi.

Several minutes later, she was at Isobel's apartment building, standing at the front door. She opened the door and headed up a flight of stairs.

Emma took a deep breath and wiped her sweating palms on her jeans.

She found apartment five and then looked through Isobel's bag for the key.

Her hands shook as she tried to hold the key. It fit the lock, and it turned with a light 'click.' She could feel her pulse in her fingers and toes.

When she stepped inside, she saw a fluffy rug and a leather couch with decorative cushions. Her fingers ran along the soft fabric of the cushions, feeling the soft tassels on the ends. None of her cushions at home were so fancy.

She wandered through the other rooms and found the apartment was exactly as described. There was one bedroom, a large wardrobe, one bathroom, a small kitchenette, and a living area.

Emma dropped onto the russet leather chair, plopping her feet on the coffee table with a thud. She was determined to enjoy having no chores for one whole week.

Emma closed her eyes and was just drifting off to sleep when a banging on her door startled her.

Who could it be? Her mother, perhaps?

Her heart thudded loudly in her ears as she tried to

recall the names of Isobel's friends from the pictures she had seen and moved to the door.

A young girl with long, straight black hair, a nose piercing, and all-black clothing stood outside the door. Emma recognized her right away as Jade, one of Isobel's friends.

"Where have you been? I've been texting you all day!" Jade swept past Emma into the living room and perched on top of the coffee table.

A chill went up Emma's spine. She realized that the one thing Isobel hadn't thought about was keeping her cell phone. It would have been better if Isobel had given Emma her old phone and kept a new one for herself.

Emma needed to come up with an excuse quickly. "I lost my phone, and I've got a new one." Emma rushed over to her bag and picked up her cell phone.

"Well, what's the number?" Jade took out her own phone from her pocket, waiting for the information.

Emma gazed down at the phone. How would she get the number? She only knew Isobel's number; she didn't even know her own. "I don't know the number."

Jade rolled her eyes in response. "You're silly. Give it to me." She grabbed Emma's phone and pressed a few buttons until her own phone rang. "I can get the number on my phone."

Emma nodded, relieved. "Great."

Jade handed Emma back her phone. "I noticed that you don't have anyone's numbers saved in here."

"I know. I haven't had time to save any numbers yet," Emma replied with a shrug.

"You should've transferred them."

"I didn't."

Jade let out a deep breath. "Okay, I'll write everyone's numbers down for you, so you can add them later. Do you have a pen and paper? Or I can text you all our friends' numbers."

"Writing them down would be better." Emma searched through drawers in the kitchen before finding paper and a pen to give Jade.

"Is everything okay, Isobel?"

"Jah." Emma immediately coughed to disguise that she had just responded in Pennsylvania Dutch. "Yes, I'm fine, just feeling a bit off. Maybe it's a cold or something."

Jade pushed out her lips while writing names and numbers from her phone.

Based on Isobel's diary, Jade was Isobel's closest friend who also studied at the same college. Jade resided with her parents and lived ten minutes away from Isobel's apartment.

As Jade scribbled away on the paper, Emma studied her - wondering how she could possibly fool Jade into thinking she was Isobel. According to what she'd read, Jade and Isobel had been friends for years, so there would have to be some hidden memories and private things that only they both knew.

Jade put the pen down and handed Emma the paper. "Oh, and happy birthday!" She leaped to her feet, offering a hug before sitting back on the coffee table in a cross-legged position. "Don't forget, you're coming out tonight."

"How could I forget? I've been looking forward to it. Where are we going again?"

"It's a secret! I'll pick you up at eleven."

Eleven? That must have been wrong. Why would someone go out that late at night? Before Emma could ask, however, Jade was already halfway out the door. It was like a mini tornado had just passed through the room.

"Bye," Emma called after her.

"Later!" Jade was already out the door and heading down the stairs.

Emma closed the door and headed to Isobel's bedroom, planning to find something more comfortable to change into. Just as she opened the wardrobe door, there was another knock on the door.

CHAPTER 9

When Isobel arrived back at the house with Hosea, she found her grandmother busy in the kitchen.

"Hello, Mrs. Byler," Hosea said.

Mammi swung around to see them both standing there. "Oh, hello, Hosea. It's good to see you."

"Can I help with anything, *Mammi*?"

"*Nee*, not when it's your birthday. You and Hosea can wait outside for the other guests."

"Are you sure?"

"*Jah*, off you go."

Isobel looked over at Hosea, who smiled and said, "We better go outside then."

Isobel gave a nod, and together they walked outside to the porch. They sat down side by side in large wooden chairs.

As Isobel watched a girl pulling up in a buggy, it led

her to wonder if she would be expected to drive a buggy and hitch it to the horse at some stage of her visit. She had no idea in the world how she would even attempt to do such a thing. Besides, she was scared of horses.

She decided then and there to Google how to hitch an Amish buggy to a horse and how to drive one; she'd do that as soon as her guests left. It was then that it dawned on Isobel that there was no electricity in the *haus*, so she would have no way of charging her laptop or her cell phone. Perhaps Hosea could drive her somewhere to find electricity.

"Happy birthday, Emma." A very plain girl ran toward Isobel, and Isobel noticed that the girl had her eyes fixed on Hosea. She wondered if this was Emma's best friend, Mary, or perhaps it could have been one of the two sisters that Emma had mentioned. No, it must have been Mary because surely the sisters would arrive together.

"Thank you," Isobel replied. "I'm glad you could come."

"Of course. I wouldn't miss it. It'll be my birthday soon, and you'll have to come to my birthday dinner." The girl didn't look at Isobel long before she looked adoringly at Hosea. "And you too, Hosea."

Hosea smiled and nodded. "*Denke*, Mary."

Ah, it is Mary. Isobel studied Mary's face. She had a wide nose to go with her wide face, and her lips were very thin. Isobel considered that her green eyes could be her best features, except they would need to be brought out with black mascara and eyeliner. Isobel was sorry for Mary; she was badly in need of a makeover.

Isobel laughed to herself. No Amish girl would ever think the things that she was thinking. She could think all of the awful things she liked, and no one would ever know. She was Amish on the outside, but on the inside, she certainly was not.

Isobel heard a loud, rumbling sound and looked up to see two buggies heading toward the house.

"Here they all are," Hosea said.

When the two girls got out of their buggy and approached the house, Isobel studied Hosea's face to see if he might be interested in either of them. He certainly was not interested in Mary, not romantically.

Isobel judged the sisters as only marginally more attractive than Mary, and they were certainly no match for herself in the looks department. She had no worries there. She had been raised by her mother to take pride in her appearance. Her mother had ensured she only ever wore the best clothes and had the best of everything, paid for, in the last few years, by her mother's boyfriend.

The two girls ran the last few steps to Isobel and kissed her on the cheek. "Happy birthday, Emma."

"*Denke*. I'm so glad you're here."

They all waited for David King, who was tying up his horse.

"You're the last one, David, as always," Hosea yelled out.

David grinned and strutted toward them. "I'm not late. I'm right on time, I'd say."

"*Jah*, you're right on time, David," Isobel said.

"Happy birthday, Emma."

"*Denke*, David." Isobel walked into the house, and her guests followed. Once they were inside, Isobel invited everyone to sit, and then she did not know what to say next. She could not ask them any questions because she knew nothing about these people. For the first time in her life, she was lost for words. "I'll just see if *Mammi* needs any help."

Isobel finally admitted to herself that swapping lives with Emma wasn't going to be as easy as she had visualized. "*Mammi*, do you need some help? Everyone's here now. Unless you invited someone else."

"I saw them from the window. They're the only people coming. I know you don't like crowds." *Mammi* had two large saucepans bubbling on the stove and was bending over to look at something in the oven. She closed the oven door and straightened up. "I've made a jug of lemonade." *Mammi* pointed to a large jug on a tray with several glasses sitting on the old wooden table. "You talk to your friends, and then you can help serve the food. The food is ten minutes away."

Isobel was pleased to have the distraction of serving her guests lemonade. "*Denke*, I'll take the lemonade out to them. Dinner smells *gut*."

Mammi's blue eyes twinkled at the compliment.

Isobel carried the heavy tray of lemonade to Emma's friends.

"I'll help you with that, Emma." Hosea leaped off the couch, took the tray away from Isobel, and placed it on the table.

"Thank you, Hosea. Does everyone want lemonade?" Isobel could not believe that she was offering lemonade to grown people. If she were to have guests to dinner in her own home, she would certainly serve them something a little stronger. Even though she was only eighteen, she and her friends had no need to follow rules. After everyone had a glass, she poured herself one and sank down on the couch next to Mary.

Isobel turned her body slightly to face Mary. "What did you do today, Mary?"

"I started sewing a quilt, a double wedding ring quilt." A look of smugness covered her face, and her thin lips curled upward.

Katie and Lizzy giggled, and Lizzy said, "Is it for you when you get married?"

Isobel noticed that the two boys looked at each other and exchanged amused looks.

Immediately Isobel felt sorry for the Amish women who had to marry so young and then have a tribe of children. It seemed so last century.

"Well," Mary began, "It's *gut* to be ready, and by the time I marry, I'll have a nice quilt for the marriage bed."

"That's a great idea," Isobel said while wondering what Emma's response might have been.

"I'll have your help now, Emma," her grandmother called from the kitchen.

Phew saved, Isobel thought as she scurried to the kitchen.

Once everyone took their seats around the table, Hosea asked, "Is this all your favorite food, Emma?"

"*Jah*, it is. I love…" Isobel hesitated as she didn't know the names of any of the dishes on the table, so she finished by saying, "All of this."

"I love the baked sweet potatoes. That's my favorite," Hosea said.

"Me too. That's my special favorite too," Isobel blurted out.

Mary didn't look too happy. "Everyone likes them."

"Not me. I like Chinese food. I had it once, and I can't wait to have it again," David said.

Isobel nearly choked on a piece of chicken when she suddenly remembered that Mom and Frank had arranged to take her out to a Chinese restaurant for her birthday. She knew that Emma would not be ready for such a test – not on her first day of being Isobel.

CHAPTER 10

"Isobel?" The voice of an older woman sounded from outside. Emma opened the door to see an older lady who looked like herself. It was hard to take her eyes off her. It had to be her mother.

"Happy birthday, sweetheart." The woman offered her cheek, and Emma kissed it, catching sight of a dark-skinned man behind her. The woman passed through the entranceway into the apartment.

"Happy birthday, Isobel." The man gave her some flowers along with a package covered in pink paper and tied with a large pink bow.

"Thank you." Emma moved aside to let him in. He had to be her mother's boyfriend, Frank.

"Did you give her the present, Frank?"

"Yes, he did, Mom. Here it is." Emma placed the flowers on a side table and sat down in a leather chair; the parcel cradled in her lap. Her mom and Frank were both across from her on the couch.

"Well, open it," her mother suggested, leaning forward in anticipation.

Emma slipped off the ribbon and tore away the paper to discover a small but stunningly polished wooden box within. She stared at it for a few moments before Frank spoke up. "The box isn't the present—you've got to open it!"

When she opened it up, there were two earrings nestled within that shone brightly when held up to the light. "Wow! They are beautiful; thank you so much."

Her mom leaned closer to observe Emma's ears more closely. "You're not wearing the earrings we got you for Christmas."

"No, I haven't put them in yet," Emma said, trying to appear nonchalant while leaning away. Her ears weren't even pierced. Isobel's were. "Thank you, Mom and Frank," Emma said again as she held up one of the earrings admiringly.

Frank grunted. "Well, they aren't exactly the ones you wanted."

"These are perfect. I love them." Emma was aware of how expensive this gift must've been, but where was her gift? She had never even gotten a birthday card from her mother. Nothing! All Emma wished for was some sort of acknowledgment of her existence. Was that too much to ask?

Her mother's eyes ran over Emma's sweatpants and

loose T-shirt as she frowned. "You're not going to wear those clothes to dinner, are you?"

"Dinner?" Emma asked.

Frank nodded. "I told you she'd forget. She's probably got something arranged already with those dreadful friends of hers."

"No, I didn't forget," Emma replied quickly. "I'll just change my clothes." As Emma went to look for something suitable to wear, she realized that she hadn't considered how she'd have to fool her mother into believing she was Isobel.

Jade had been fooled, but her own mother might not be so easy.

To her surprise, her mother followed her into the bedroom. "I think it would be best if I choose something for you to wear. Frank gets angry when you dress like a homeless person." She opened the wardrobe and proceeded to throw items onto the bed. "I wish you wouldn't wear jeans all the time. You must have about fifty pairs."

"Sorry, Mom."

Her mother swung around to face her. "Are you feeling all right, Isobel? You're just not yourself, are you?"

Emma shrugged. "I guess I'm feeling a little off today."

"Have you been drinking again?"

Emma shook her head. "No, Mom."

"Hmmm." Her mother studied her and then turned her attention back to the clothes. "Okay, you can choose anything I put on the bed."

Emma looked at the bundle of clothes. She chose a light pink shirt and a black skirt. She wondered if Isobel would've objected to her mom picking her clothes for her. Her mother sat on the edge of the bed while Emma changed into the new outfit. "Hurry up, or Frank will be mad that we're late."

Emma figured it wasn't the best time to push boundaries with her mom over clothing choices, even though Isobel may have done so.

Emma found some black shoes in the cupboard with high heels, but after putting them on she found she couldn't walk in them. Thankfully, Isobel had a large selection, so Emma found a pair with a lower heel. "How's this, Mom?"

Her mother laughed. "That's an improvement. A lot better than you usually wear. Show Frank."

Emma walked out into the living room.

"What do you think, Frank?" her mother asked.

Frank was looking at his phone and looked up as soon as he heard his name. "What?"

"Will you get off that phone for once, Frank? You're turning it off when we get to the restaurant."

He slid his phone into his pocket.

"That's better. I said, what do you think about what Isobel's wearing?"

He looked Emma up and down. "That'll do fine."

Her mom stood up. "Let's go."

As Emma walked toward the front door, her mom asked, "Aren't you going to wear your birthday earrings?"

A chill ran up Emma's spine. She did not have holes in her ears, and these earrings were obviously for someone with pierced ears. "No, they're too special, and I might lose them. I'll leave them here where they'll be safe."

Mom peered into her face very closely. "You do like them, don't you?"

"Yes, Mom. I love them. Of course, I do. Who wouldn't?"

"Rose, she's been nagging for them for a year; I'm sure she likes them. Well, they're nearly as big as the ones she's been nagging for. Can we go before we lose our booking at the restaurant?" Frank strode toward the door.

Her mom lifted Emma's long hair away from her ears. "The holes in your ears have closed. Haven't you been wearing any earrings at all?"

Emma pulled her hair over her ears. "Not for a while."

Her mother frowned. "That was silly. Now you'll have to have them pierced again."

"Okay, I'll do it later."

Her mother gasped. "What do you mean? You can't do it yourself. That's very unhygienic. What's wrong with teenagers these days?"

Emma was not sure about pierced ears and did not know why she couldn't do it. Neither was she quite sure of what it entailed. Emma shrugged her shoulders. "Okay, I won't do it myself."

Her mother looked up at Frank, who was looking bored.

Frank shook his head. "See, I told you things like this would happen if we left her by herself."

"I blame those friends of hers," her mother grumbled.

Frank held the door open for them and said, "I suppose she has to grow up and start looking after herself sometime. Meaning, we can't choose her friends for her."

"Hmm. More's the pity," Mom commented.

"Isobel, I put the flowers in water for you."

"Thank you, Frank. I meant to do that. The flowers are beautiful. I'll enjoy them."

"We know roses are your favorite," Mom commented.

"They sure are." Emma smiled. It was another thing that she shared with Isobel.

CHAPTER 11

Hosea looked over at Isobel. "You're very lively tonight."

"Am I? I guess I'm a little tired, and I get overactive when I'm like this."

Mammi chuckled. "Must have been the day free from chores. Staying in bed sleeping half the day just makes a person sleepier."

"I guess so." Again, Isobel agreed with her grandmother. "It's my birthday, and I can do anything I like, even sleep all day. I only slept half the day, and I enjoyed every minute of it." Isobel giggled a little.

David stared at her and tilted his head slightly to one side. "I saw something very funny today."

"What was it?" asked Mary.

"I saw a person who looked very much like you, Emma. She got into a taxi at the end of the street."

Isobel remembered that Emma had said that David

lived close by. He must have seen Emma leaving. "Well, it wasn't me. I was home all morning and then went for a walk." And that was the truth.

David was not going to let this go. "I could have sworn it was you, except it was an *Englisher*."

Isobel giggled loudly. "Well, I'm not an *Englisher*."

Mary unknowingly saved the day as she interrupted the conversation. "Are you going on *rumspringa*, Hosea?"

Hosea swallowed his mouthful and then answered, "*Nee*; I'm not much interested in the English world. Seems to be just a lot of bother and a lot of temptations."

"*Jah*, why put yourself in the way of temptation?" David stated. "I'm not going either."

"*Rumspringa* is not just temptations. It's a way to find out the reasons why you want to remain in the community. No *gut* staying if your heart isn't in it. People who have been on *rumspringa* never have regrets and are never left wondering about the English world," Isobel's grandmother said.

"Did you go on *rumspringa*, Mrs. Byler?" Lizzy asked.

"*Nee*, it was not around in my day."

Lizzy helped herself to more dumplings. It seemed she was more interested in the food than being involved in the conversation.

"So, you would let Emma go on *rumspringa*?" Mary asked.

"*Jah*, if she wanted to, of course." *Mammi* nodded.

Isobel looked at Mary and wondered why she would ask such a thing. From one conversation with Emma, she was sure that Emma was not having second thoughts about being Amish.

Isobel wondered if any of Emma's friends sitting around the table had part-time jobs. Maybe Emma had mentioned it to her, but she could not recall. Of course, she couldn't ask. That was something that she should have known. Isobel vaguely recalled Emma saying that the two sisters had part-time jobs.

"Why so deep in thought, Emma?"

Isobel looked up to see Hosea's warm eyes fixed upon her. "Just wishing I could have a part-time job, that's all." She shot a look at her grandmother.

Mammi leaned toward her. "When you're older. We've already discussed it, Emma."

It did not make sense to Emma that her grandmother did not want her to have a part-time job but did not mind if she went on *rumspringa*. It seemed contradictory.

Isobel finished her dinner in silence, lost in thought about what her grandmother had said.

"If I'm honest," Mary began, "I've always felt a little trapped in this small community, and the idea of going out into the English world is tempting. But it would mean leaving behind everything I know, like my family and my friends. It's a scary thought."

Everyone was quiet, and all eyes were on Mary. Isobel could feel the tension in the air. It was as if everyone was waiting for Mary to say something more. Mary remained silent, staring down at her plate as though lost in thought.

Mammi broke the silence. "It's understandable, Mary.

The outside world can be a scary place, but staying here just because it's familiar is not a good enough reason to keep you from exploring the world if you're curious."

David nodded in agreement. "Sometimes I am curious, but like Mary said, leaving everything is daunting even if it's just going to be for a while."

Isobel had never really thought that Amish people would want to explore the world or be curious about it. She'd just imagined they'd be happy where they were, and that was that. "Maybe there's a way for you to have the best of both worlds," Isobel said.

"What do you mean?" David asked.

"I mean, maybe there's a way for someone to experience the *English* world without leaving your family and friends behind," Isobel explained.

Mary looked intrigued. "How would that work?"

"Well, you could get a job and work for an *Englisher*. That way, you'll experience a different way of life, but you still have your family and friends in the Amish community."

Mammi interrupted their conversation. "Enough talk of the *English* world. It's getting late, and we all have chores to do in the morning, I'm sure."

Isobel frowned. Everyone had only just finished their meal.

Isobel looked at Mary sympathetically. At their age, they should be able to do anything they liked.

As they all got up to leave the table, Hosea touched Isobel's arm. "You're a wise woman, Emma. I think you're onto something there." He gave her a smile before walking away.

Warmth spread through her whole body at his touch.

Isobel followed everyone outside and thanked them all for coming.

"We had a *wunderbaar* time, Emma," Mary said.

Hosea leaned in close. "I'll see you soon then, Emma."

"You will?" Mary said, "When will you see her?"

Isobel nearly gasped at Mary's outspokenness.

"That is between Emma and me," Hosea spoke politely and walked slowly to his waiting buggy, leaving Mary standing next to Isobel.

"What did he mean by that, Emma?" Mary's bottom jaw jutted out as she glared at Isobel. "You know that I like him."

"Mary, I don't want to argue with you again, but you know that I like him too, right?" Isobel was not going to back down, and it was quite clear that Hosea preferred her to Mary. "I'm sorry Mary, but he's driving me home from the next singing."

Mary turned and left without saying another word.

Mammi joined Isobel at the door while she waved to the last of her friends as they drove off. Isobel closed her eyes and listened to the clip-clopping of the horses' hooves.

"Did you have a good day?" *Mammi* asked.

"*Denke, Mammi,* that was a lovely dinner."

"It's a special birthday. You go to bed; I'll clean up the kitchen."

"*Nee*, I'll help you. There are so many dishes," Isobel said.

"Off you go, birthday girl, and tomorrow it's back to normal."

Isobel wondered just what 'normal' would be. "Are you sure you don't want help?"

"*Jah*. I can do it by myself." *Mammi* gave her a hug.

Emma had told her she had to be up early to start the chores. She hadn't even had time to look at the kitchen chores list. How was she going to wake up without an alarm clock? She could use the alarm on her phone, but *Mammi* might hear it. "I insist on helping. It's only fair."

Mammi chuckled. "Okay."

As Isobel scrubbed the dishes, she realized she had enjoyed socializing with Emma's friends. They were different from her usual crowd, but something about their sincerity allowed her to be herself -- even if she was pretending to be someone else.

Isobel pondered when she'd see Hosea again. He had promised to give her a ride home after the singing, but where and when would that be?

CHAPTER 12

"We're taking you to your favorite Chinese restaurant if you still want to go there," Mom said as soon as the three of them piled into a taxi.

Emma gasped. "Oh yes, I love Chinese food."

"That's why we're taking you there." Frank's tone was dry, and Emma wondered if he was always so bored with everything.

Emma had been to a Chinese restaurant near her home twice, and she loved the food. She was amazed and delighted that her twin loved the same kind of food as she.

When they entered the restaurant, Emma noticed it was grander than the Chinese restaurant she'd been to before. Everywhere she looked, there were red and gold decorations, from wall-to-wall paintings to little golden statues here and there. She wondered if these figurines were what the bishop had referred to as graven images; however, she resisted looking at them for too long.

A waitress in a heavily embroidered dress led them to their table. As they studied the menus, Mom said, "I hope you do just as well in your college courses during this second half of the year."

Before she could answer, Frank chimed in, "She'd better."

Emma's mother shot Frank a look, which told him to keep quiet, and then she continued, "It's just that you're getting an opportunity that I never had, and I wouldn't like you to waste it." She leaned in close. "I know you're upset about that young man, but don't let that distract you from your studies."

"I won't, Mom. He's just a boy. I mean, a young man. I'll do well; you'll see."

"Good."

Frank looked down at his menu. "Let's order; I'm starving."

Mom rolled her eyes. "You're always starving."

Frank ignored the remark.

Emma was pleased that she'd come this far without her mother realizing she was not Isobel. While she looked at the choices on the menu, she wondered how Isobel was getting along at the birthday dinner. She hoped that Isobel was keeping Mary away from Hosea. Not that she felt that Mary was a threat, but any woman was a threat when it came to Hosea since every girl in the County was in love with him.

As Emma perused the menu, her eyes landed on an item she had never seen before. It was called "firecracker shrimp," and it sounded dangerously spicy. Despite her curiosity, she hesitated to order it. She was never one for spicy food, but something about the name intrigued her.

Before she could decide, Frank spoke up. "We'll have the firecracker shrimp as an appetizer. And I'll have the mixed omelet with a few of your different sauces." He handed the menu back to the waitress, who'd just come back to the table.

Mom nodded in agreement. "Have you decided yet, Isobel?"

"Um, not yet," Emma replied, quickly scanning the page before her. "Everything looks so good."

"I know, right?" Frank grinned. "I was thinking about getting the kung pao chicken."

"I was thinking the same thing. Yes, I'll have that," Emma said, relieved that she had help to decide.

"I'll have something different so we can share." Mom closed her menu. "How about the moo shu pork?"

"Sounds good, Mom," Emma said with a smile.

"That's everything then?" asked the waitress.

"Yes," Frank answered.

Once the waitress left, Mom struck up a conversation about college and what she hoped Emma would accomplish in her remaining time there.

Emma tried to listen, but her mind kept drifting to Hosea. She couldn't help but wonder what he was doing now.

Was he thinking about her?

Did he miss her? Of course, he wouldn't. Isobel was there in her place.

She shook her head, trying to push those thoughts from her mind. She was here with her family, and she needed to focus on the present. She hoped Mom wouldn't be mad at her if she ever learned who she really was.

Emma reminded herself that she should be the one who was angry. Mom had left her with *Mammi* and, for all Emma knew, had never looked back.

Just then, their appetizer arrived, and Emma's attention was drawn back to the table. The firecracker shrimp looked as delicious as it sounded, but Emma hesitated. She wasn't sure if she could handle the heat.

"It looks amazing," Emma's mother said, reaching for a shrimp. She popped it into her mouth and closed her eyes in delight. "Oh my goodness, this is so good! You have to try it, Isobel."

Frank nodded in agreement. "It's not too spicy, but it definitely has a kick to it."

Emma took a deep breath and picked up a shrimp. She closed her eyes and savored the explosion of flavors in her mouth. It was spicy but not overwhelmingly so, and the shrimp was perfectly cooked. She opened her eyes and smiled. "This is amazing," she said, reaching for another shrimp.

They finished the appetizer quickly, and soon their mains arrived. Emma's kung pao chicken was exactly what she had hoped it would be—spicy, savory, and delicious. She savored each bite.

Emma's mind ran away with her again, back to Hosea. The thought of Mary throwing herself at him made her stomach churn with jealousy.

As the dinner went on, Emma found it harder and harder to stay focused. She had to get home as soon as she could. Seven more days to go.

"Is everything okay, Isobel?" Her mother's voice snapped her out of her thoughts. "You've been awfully quiet tonight."

Emma forced a smile. "Yeah, I'm fine. I'm just tired from studying."

"I suppose that's the best reason to be tired." Her mother gave her a concerned look but didn't press the issue.

Emma stared at her mother. Had she given *her* one thought after she left her with *Mammi?* Did she spare one moment today to wonder what Emma was doing?

CHAPTER 13

Isobel needed some type of lamp to take to her bedroom. There was a large overhead gas lamp in the kitchen and one in the main living room, but the rest of the *haus,* except for the kitchen, was in darkness.

She spied two small kerosene lamps, like the ones she had seen in antique shops, sitting on a table in the corner of the room. She picked up one of the lamps but had no idea how to light it. There was only one thing she could do.

Isobel carried the lamp into the kitchen. "Could you light this for me, *Mammi?*"

Mammi laughed. "Why?"

Isobel murmured something about forgetting how to do it.

"Are you all right, Emma?" Her grandmother put the back of her hand on Isobel's forehead. "You don't feel like you've got a temperature." She took the lamp from Isobel.

"Give it here then." She lit it at the top with a match. "Too hard for you, eh?"

Isobel smiled. *"Denke.* I get a little scared of matches sometimes. Good night, *Mammi."*

"Good night, Emma, and happy birthday."

"Denke." Isobel walked up the stairs with her lamp lighting the way. Once Isobel was inside Emma's bedroom, she reached under the pillow for her cell phone. She saw by the flashing screen that her cell phone battery was nearly dead. Then, she realized she had no way of charging it because there was no electricity in the *haus.*

She ignored a bunch of texts from Jade that had come yesterday and checked for missed calls. There were none. By that, she assumed that Emma was all right and that she'd managed to fool everyone.

The time on the phone said nine o'clock, which apparently, by Amish standards, was late. There was no way she could fall asleep this early no matter what time she was supposed to get up the next morning.

She set the kerosene lamp on the nightstand and looked around Emma's room for something to read. The only thing she could find was a pattern book for quilts. She grabbed it and lay down on the bed. It was only then she had a better look at the quilt on Emma's bed. She recalled Emma had said it had been made by Mammi.

Isobel picked up the edge of the quilt and studied the fine stitches. It looked like a store-bought quilt. Isobel had never been interested in needlework or sewing, but as she looked through the handsome and intricate patterns in the book, she wanted to have a go at sewing her very own quilt. In the book, she found a picture of the double wedding ring quilt that Mary had talked about. Isobel admired pictures of the other traditional quilts, the wedding star, a tumbling block quilt, and the broken star quilt.

Isobel's eyes grew tired, and she checked on her phone to see what time it was. It was one minute past midnight. Still early by her standards, but maybe she should try to sleep.

She studied the lamp and tried to figure out how to snuff the flames. Was it like a candle that she should snuff or blow out the flame? She noticed a little screw-like thing on the side and turned it, causing the flame to go out.

Immediately, Isobel was scared because she was engulfed in a blanket of darkness. There were no streetlights or neon signs. Not only was it pitch black, it was deadly silent. It was as though nothing in the world existed. She closed her eyes, thinking about what she was doing with her life until sleep overtook her.

CHAPTER 14

*E*mma considered that her first meeting with her mother and Frank had gone well. Neither Frank nor her mom had any clue who she was. She'd had an entire meal with them at a restaurant and nothing bad had happened. That gave her confidence that she would be able to last the week. Isobel would be happy about that.

The taxi pulled up at Isobel's apartment. Emma looked over at her mother.

Mom said, "We won't come up, we'll keep going. We're staying overnight in town. We'll call you tomorrow and we can have brunch together if you'd like."

"That would be good." Emma remembered the phone mix-up, and then added, "I have a new phone number, Mom."

"You'd better give it to me."

Frank handed Emma a pen and she found a slip of

paper in her handbag, and she wrote down the number for her mom. "There you go."

"Thank you. Bye, darling." Her mom stuck out her cheek and Emma kissed it before she got out of the taxi.

Once Emma was on the pavement, she leaned over and said goodbye to Frank, who was sitting on the other side. "Bye, see you in the morning."

Emma watched the taxi speed away. Her mom seemed to be loving and kind, but why had she left her all that time with *Mammi* and never even visited? Had she been such a horrible child that her mother didn't even want to remember that she had another daughter?

As she was about to enter the building, another taxi pulled up. She paid no attention until she heard someone calling out Isobel's name. She turned to see Isobel's friend, Jade, who had been at the apartment earlier.

Every muscle in Emma's body was drained of energy. How she longed to be able to collapse into her very own bed at home, back in Lancaster County.

"Are you ready? We can go in this taxi," Jade said.

Emma wondered if she should tell Jade that she wasn't feeling well, but she did want an adventure and that's why she had come here in the first place. Emma would have just gone to sleep, but obviously, Isobel would have gone out with her friends.

"Yes, I'm ready." Emma shrugged off her tiredness and smiled as she got into the backseat of the taxi with Jade. "Where are we going?"

"A few of us are meeting at a club, apart from that, it's a surprise."

Emma was silent. A club? Was that like a restaurant? She had eaten all she could already. She wondered how she would eat more since she was not a big eater.

Emma closed her eyes for a moment and wondered how Isobel had gotten along with her friends back home. She knew that everyone at home would be fast asleep by now. Home was so peaceful in comparison with the bright lights of New York; it appeared as though no one in New York slept at all. Even through her closed eyelids, Emma could still see the bright lights as the taxi drove past every manner of streetlight and flashing sign.

"You okay, Isobel?" Jade clutched her arm.

"Yes, a little tired. I've just come back from going out to dinner with Mom and Frank."

"Well, I hope you're still hungry. We're eating first."

"Yes. I've been looking forward to it." Emma grimaced in the dark seat of the taxi; she had just told another lie.

The taxi pulled up outside the restaurant, and Jade threw the driver some money and pulled Emma out of the car. Jade hooked her arm through Emma's and ushered her through the doors of the restaurant. They stopped at a table where three girls were sitting, waiting. Emma recognized all the young women from Isobel's notebook. Emma had memorized their names, but now she was face to face with them, their names left her head completely.

The girls welcomed Emma with a flurry of hugs and birthday wishes. As soon as she was seated, Emma knew it would be a long and tiresome night. "I'll be right back," she said as she stood to go to the restroom.

Once inside, she reached into her bag and checked her mobile phone. Nothing had changed since the last time she looked—no missed calls.

On her way back to the table, Emma noticed a man walking toward her. Something about his confident gait and bright eyes made him stand out from the crowd.

"Isobel." The man lunged at her arm and took hold of it just above her wrist. His grip was firm, firm enough to hurt Emma a little.

"Stop it." Emma tried to free herself from him, but his strong hand had a firm hold on her tiny arm. "Let me go or I'll scream."

The handsome stranger released her arm immediately. "Sorry. I just want to speak with you."

Emma rubbed her wrist, which was burning from his touch. "Why?" Her tone was angry, and her lips pouted her disapproval of this man's manners.

He planted his feet solidly on the floor, and his hands lay gently on his hips as he softly said, "I just want to say I'm sorry for everything you think I've done."

Emma's eyes ran up and down him. This had to be Travis, the man who upset Isobel so badly. There was nothing about Travis in the notebook. Had Isobel thought she wouldn't run into him?

"It was a terrible thing that you thought I did, and I would like you to forgive me if you can." His soft brown eyes burned straight into hers.

If only Isobel had said what this man had done to her. She only said that he broke her heart, but it was enough to make her cry and run away, away from New York. "I'm not sure." Emma's speech was stammered. "I'll have to think about it."

Emma's heart raced, and her breathing became shallow. She needed to be outside, away from this crowded place. Emma turned her back on him to return to her waiting friends when Travis grabbed her shoulders, which made her gasp for air, but the more she gasped, the less air became available.

Emma clutched at her throat as she fought for air. Was she dying? Was this *Gott's* punishment for deceiving her mom and her grandmother, and all the other people? A crowd gathered around her.

"Call 911." Emma heard someone say.

"Isobel, are you okay?" Travis asked, leaning over her.

She heard Jade's voice. "Get away from her, Travis. See what you've done? Just go away."

Emma looked up to see Jade pushing him away.

Then Emma heard someone say he was a doctor. "She's having a panic attack. Possibly hyperventilating." Someone gave the doctor a paper bag. "Breathe into this." The doctor held the bag over her face.

As she breathed into the bag, her breathing stabilized in a matter of moments.

"She's breathing normally. Thank you, doctor," Jade said.

The doctor took hold of Emma's wrist and checked her

pulse. "She'll probably be okay, but I strongly suggest you take her to the hospital and have them run some tests."

"I'll take her straight there," Travis said.

"No, I will," Jade insisted.

The doctor stood between them. "This won't help her. Why don't you both take her?"

Travis helped Emma to her feet. "C'mon, let's get you to the hospital."

CHAPTER 15

*E*mma dozed on the hospital bed. She had never been to a hospital before or even a doctor. Her grandmother always said that a dose of castor oil cured all ills, and that's exactly what Emma had been given whenever she was unwell. It was for that very reason that she never let *Mammi* know when she was feeling off-color. The only thing that Emma liked about castor oil was the blue bottles that it came in.

An elderly doctor in a long, white coat pulled back the curtain. "Everything appears to be okay. It seems you had a panic attack. I'll give you the number of someone you can talk with. I'm sure that will help. Have you had panic attacks before?"

"No, I've never had anything like it."

"It's not unusual. Maybe you will never have another." The doctor looked down and scribbled something on his paperwork, then looked up. "You're free to leave as soon as you wish."

"Thank you."

As soon as the doctor left, Emma changed out of her hospital gown.

Jade flung open the curtains that surrounded her bed. "What's going on, Isobel?"

Emma looked into Jade's worried face. "What do you mean?"

"Something's not right with you. Please tell me what's happening?"

"I don't know what you're talking about, Jade. They said I had a panic attack, and it's nothing serious." Emma's heart was pumping faster, and she hoped that she would not have another panic attack or possibly even a heart attack.

"No, I don't mean that. I was looking for your mom's number so I could tell her that you're in the hospital and I came across this book." She threw Isobel's notebook on the table. "You've written everything down about your life. Are you having trouble with your memory?"

Emma closed her eyes tightly and put her hand up to her head. "Sometimes, well... a little." Emma was at first horrified that Jade had found the book, but losing her memory was a perfect excuse for when she got something wrong.

"That could be serious, Isobel. Did you tell the doctor?"

"No. I'm sure it's not important. I've just got too many

things to remember. My brain can only hold so much before things start falling off the edges. You know, like when you fill up a glass so full that it goes over the edge."

"You should tell the doctor. I'll fetch him."

"No," Emma spoke firmly. As she examined Jade's disapproving face, she added, "I will go to another doctor, if it continues. I just want to get out of here. It is my birthday."

Jade looked doubtful.

"I mean it, Jade. I had a memory problem a while ago, but I've been good for a long while. I think it's just too much studying." She licked her lips. "And stress over Travis." Emma knew she should not be telling so many lies, but in the position she was in, she didn't know what else to do. If she didn't tell so many lies, everyone would find out that she wasn't really Isobel. If that happened, she'd have to go home early and disappoint Isobel.

Jade pressed her lips tightly together. "You could be right. You do study far too much. I've already told you that, and I also told you that Travis is no good. I really liked him, but not now you told me what he did."

"Where's Travis? Is he still here?"

Jade rolled her eyes. "Him – he's out in the waiting room. He's pretending he cares about you – after what he's done. Why don't you tell him to go away?"

"I suppose I could." Emma found Travis to be a pleasant person, especially since he had apologized for whatever wrong he had done. She knew it was the right thing to do to forgive people. Even though she was curious about what he had done, Emma decided it would be better to save her questions to Jade about more pressing matters than a man. "You didn't tell my mother anything, did you?"

"No, I was just about to before I saw your notebook."

"That's good; I don't want her getting worried."

"Yeah, that's understandable. She does tend to stress quite a bit."

Jade's comment both surprised and disappointed Emma. Why would her mother worry so much about Isobel and not give a care in the world about her?

CHAPTER 16

"*E*mma! Whatever is the matter with you?" Isobel opened one eye and saw her grandmother's mouth opening and closing. She pulled the pillow over her face to shut out the light.

"It's time to get up," *Mammi* stated.

Isobel sat up in bed. "The sun's barely up." Isobel held her head; she knew she shouldn't say such things. If she was going to pretend to be Emma, she needed to do what Emma usually did. Apparently, that was to get up unusually early in the morning. She wasn't sure if she could do it.

"Are you unwell?" Her grandmother leaned over her and peered into her face.

"*Nee*, it's just the excitement of my birthday yesterday."

"No. I think you might be coming down with something. You don't look very well. Stay in bed for a bit longer. When you come downstairs, I'll give you a dose of castor oil."

Castor oil? Had she heard correctly? Maybe castor oil? What was that? Isobel put her head back into the pillow. "I think you're right. A few more hours of sleep will make me feel better. Good night, *Mammi*."

"You're smiling. I don't believe you're ill now."

"I never said I was. I said there was too much excitement yesterday." Isobel sat up. The last thing she wanted was to get on the wrong side of her grandmother.

"Perhaps you need to eat. I noticed yesterday that you'd lost weight. I'll have to fatten you up with a cooked breakfast. No more cereal for you. Get dressed and I'll see you downstairs."

Isobel threw back the covers and stepped over to the window. She drew back the curtains to let the dim morning light in. "The sun's not even up," she murmured as she leaned on the windowsill, looking across the fields.

Then Isobel changed out of her nightdress and got into one of Emma's dresses. Today, she chose the brown dress, hoping it would complement her blue eyes. But who would notice? Unless Hosea visited.

She remembered Hosea asked to drive her home from the next singing, but how was she going to find out when that was, and how would she get there? "First things first. I need to get through this day of chores, and whatever this castor oil thing is."

Several moments later, she heard her grandmother's voice. "Breakfast is ready!

Isobel had only just managed to put her apron on over her dress, and she still hadn't done her hair. She quickly coiled her hair on top of her head, fastened it with pins, and fixed the white prayer *kapp* in place. Then she headed downstairs.

Mammi was already seated at the table with two meals ready. Isobel felt a bit guilty for making her wait, so she settled in to eat without another word. She eyed the bacon and eggs with heavily buttered toast hungrily. When she looked up at her grandmother, she noticed she had closed her eyes.

Isobel had nearly forgotten to observe the silent prayer before eating. Isobel closed her eyes and waited a moment before opening them again.

Mammi wasted no time starting the meal. "We should do the laundry first and then go on to gardening," *Mammi* said between mouthfuls.

Isobel wondered what kind of washer and dryer they could use without electricity as she nodded. Isobel noticed her grandmother's hands were large and thick, likely because of the heavy work she did each day. In comparison, Isobel's hands were soft, having been manicured regularly. She'd removed the acrylic nails the day before she arrived, so now her nails were short but nicely kept.

"Don't forget to milk Bessy, okay?"

"I won't forget." Isobel put her knife and fork together on the plate.

"Collected the eggs yet?"

Her grandmother would've known she'd only just got

out of bed. "*Nee.* You know I just woke up so I haven't done anything yet."

"I'm just making a point." *Mammi* shook her head and said, "You'd better go and do those things now before we start the washing."

"I will."

Her grandmother carried their empty plates to the sink and rinsed them out.

Isobel guessed that was her cue to milk Bessy, who she guessed was a cow. Collecting eggs didn't sound hard, but milking a cow was something else. At least the old woman had forgotten about giving her the castor oil.

"I just have to get something from my room first. I'll be right back." Isobel raced to her room and found her phone. She hardly had any battery left, but hopefully, she would have just enough to ask Emma how to milk a cow.

Emma answered the phone within two rings. "Hello?"

CHAPTER 17

"Emma," Isobel hissed. "I've got to milk Bessy. Where is she and how do I milk a cow?"

Emma yawned. "Oh, I'm so tired I had a terrible night, just dreadful."

"Emma, I don't have time for complaints. *Mammi* will be on to me if I don't find out how to milk a cow. You've gotta help me out!"

"Bessy's a goat, not a cow."

"A goat? Well, whatever – how do I milk her?" Isobel was agitated and tried to speak quickly in case her phone ran out of charge.

"Just inside the door of the barn is a milk bucket, and Bessy is in a pen behind the barn. Put your thumb and your forefinger up the top of the teat, where she's bagged up, and drag down toward the end. Bessy gets a little testy at first if she's really bagged up."

"Okay, thumb, forefinger and drag down?"

"Jah."

Isobel wondered how Emma had done with meeting their mom. "Okay, thanks. How are things there? Did you meet Mom?"

"*Jah*, I met her and Frank. I also met Jade and some of your other friends, including Travis."

Isobel's blood ran cold. "Travis?"

"*Jah*, he seems really nice."

A pang of jealousy shuddered through Isobel's body at the thought of her twin spending time with Travis. And she must've been spending time with him to say that he was nice.

She'd told Emma that he was awful, and he'd broken her heart. "Emma, I need to ask you to please stay there for a few more weeks. Or a few months. Please stay until I contact you again. I will look after things here. Then I'll come there and swap places back with you."

"I can't. That's too long."

"Okay. I'll come sooner than I planned, but it will be more than a week. Please say yes. I need you to stay there. It's so important that you stay until I get there. Then we'll swap back."

"All right then, as long as you—"

At that moment, the phone battery on Isobel's cell phone went dead.

"Travis is not nice!" Isobel said angrily into her phone. Then a thought occurred to Isobel. If her twin was enjoying Travis's company, Emma couldn't complain about her spending time with Hosea. She was certainly enjoying his company.

Isobel rushed downstairs and out to the barn to try milking the goat. As she searched for the bucket, Isobel wondered if she had just drank goats' milk that morning in her coffee.

She spotted the bucket close to the doorway and then moved around the back of the barn to find the goat.

The white animal watched her cautiously as Isobel circled closer. "It's all right," she uttered, somewhat nervous. She was not certain if goats bit or kicked. "If Emma can do it, then so can I," she said aloud. "Good goaty. Come here. I won't hurt you so please don't hurt me."

The goat stepped forward while Isobel put the bucket beneath her. Bessy was completely motionless as Isobel crouched to do what Emma had taught her. It took a couple of tries, but eventually, the milk started flowing. Once she'd finished milking, Isobel took the bucket inside to *Mammi*.

"Thank you." *Mammi* poured the milk into containers and glanced over at Isobel. "Now, where are those eggs?"

"I'm collecting them right now," Isobel responded.

"Before you do that, why don't you take a seat?"

Isobel obeyed and *Mammi* sat across from her.

"You've been off all day, since yesterday. Do you want to tell me what's going on?" *Mammi's* blue eyes were full of worry.

Isobel searched her grandmother's face. Had she

somehow found out about the swap? "Nothing, *Mammi*. Everything is fine," Isobel muttered as she bit down on her bottom lip and contemplated having to go back to New York early.

"You can't fool me, young lady," *Mammi* chided while shaking a finger at Isobel.

"How did you know?"

"I've told you many times before; not telling the truth is just another way of lying," *Mammi* replied sternly.

Isobel didn't have anything to say that wouldn't sound like an excuse, so she remained quiet.

"You should've mentioned that you liked Hosea earlier. His grandmother has been telling me for ages that she wants you two to get married."

Isobel could breathe again. "Oh, is that what you mean?"

"Yes."

Her secret was still safe! "I'm sorry I didn't tell you sooner. I just wanted to keep it to myself."

"We promised each other we would never keep secrets. Remember?"

Isobel drew in a deep breath. "Yes." She realized then Emma hadn't respected this promise to her grandmother. Isobel was seeing that there was more to Emma than the sweet girl she'd met.

"Hosea will make an excellent husband. His family is close to ours. His grandmother and I have known each other since we were young girls."

"I know."

"Has he told you that he likes you?"

Isobel could barely keep the smile off her face. "Hosea asked if he could drive me home from the next singing. I guess that's a good sign that he's interested."

Mammi clasped her hands together and leaned forward, a twinkle in her eye. "That's *wunderbaar*."

Isobel giggled at the way her grandmother was so happy.

"I'll take you there on Sunday, and he can bring you home."

"Oh, would you? That would be great ... *wunderbaar*." Isobel was really starting to like her *grandmother*. Now the problem was solved about how to get to the singing and when it will be held.

That night, Isobel threw herself into bed at what she figured must have been around eight o'clock. Her fingers were raw from washing the clothes by hand and feeding the clothes through the wringer that squeezed out the moisture.

Her head thumped from sheer exhaustion. The only thing she found relatively easy was the dusting. She was also sure she was allergic to something in the garden, though, as she could not stop sneezing.

Even though her fingers and shoulders ached, Isobel was certain that the very worst thing she'd done was shovel the horse manure out of the stalls.

She held up her hands and turned them and as she did, she saw little nicks and cuts from pulling weeds out of the garden. They were a little better once *Mammi* gave her some lavender oil, which she had made from their very own lavender bushes.

As she closed her eyes, a little smile crept to the corners of her mouth as she thought about Hosea. There was a connection with him from the moment she'd seen him in the fields.

Apart from all Isobel's scrapes and cuts, everything in her life was improving, and no one suspected a thing, not even *Mammi*.

She hoped that all the sneezing she was doing would not give her a red nose or red eyes for the singing tomorrow evening. Isobel wanted to be the most beautiful woman there. She was certainly going to be taken home by the most beautiful man.

There was something peaceful and grounding about being in the country and putting her hands into the soil. The soil gave life to everything.

She wondered again how Emma was getting along. Isobel was a little concerned that Emma thought Travis was 'nice.' She'd soon find out he wasn't nice, and it would serve her right for not listening to the truth about him.

Isobel's mind wandered to more serious matters, such as how she was going to get her laptop and cell phone charged. Maybe she could recharge her things at a library or some similar public place. Her wonderings reminded her that to get to such places she would need to learn to hitch the buggy and learn to drive one as well unless she wanted to be stuck at home for the next few months.

CHAPTER 18

*E*mma opened her eyes and looked around. She hoped it was all a bad dream, but no, it was real. She was pretending to be her twin and she was stuck in New York City until Isobel came to save her.

Emma had to admit that she liked the cozy apartment. Everything was clean, fresh, and bright. It was hard to keep the floor of the *haus* at home clean with walking in and out all the time. Even though she and *Mammi* changed their shoes at the doorway, the dirt always managed to find a way in.

She jumped out of bed and looked at her reflection in the bathroom mirror. Her hair stuck out in all directions, and she had massive dark circles under her eyes.

Emma looked down at the phone that was plugged into the outlet. There were still no missed calls from Isobel, not even a text.

Since Emma had to start Isobel's classes very soon, she

hoped Isobel would find somewhere to recharge her phone. If they talked on the phone about each other's lives, it would be a way to grow closer.

~

Mammi had driven to the Sunday meeting. Isobel had found out there was a singing afterward and that's what she was looking forward to so she could spend more time with Hosea.

When they pulled up, Isobel was surprised to see what looked like a hundred young people in attendance. She hadn't realized the community was so large.

Two girls came running up to meet Isobel; they were the sisters from Emma's birthday dinner. They linked arms with Isobel and took her into the crowd while *Mammi* secured the horse and buggy.

Isobel scanned the place until she saw Hosea talking idly to Mary. His eyes were searching and wandering until they landed on Isobel, and then he flashed her his best smile as if Mary didn't even exist at that moment.

The girls pulled her to a seat, and she sat down on one of the wooden benches. Before she could spend time with Hosea, she had to sit through the meeting on hard seats. The meeting was long, and everything was said in German. She spoke a little German, but still, it was hard to follow.

Isobel observed that the dresses of the Amish girls were all green, brown, yellow or burgundy, with no reds, oranges, or pinks. She understood how they dressed so similarly to fit in, as it was important that none of them stood out from one another.

Isobel reflected on how she bought her clothes – buying in bulk instead of making piece by piece like these girls had done. All their clothing was plain and simple, but when you looked closely, you could tell they had put great care and effort into making each item unique. Even their prayer *kapps* were different – some were stiff with pleats while others had soft fabric with gathers at the back. The garments initially seemed similar, but Isobel noticed individual quirks on closer inspection.

After the meeting, everyone stayed back for a meal and enjoyed a time of fellowship. Then the older folks left, leaving the young to enjoy their time of singing.

When the singing began, Mary sat behind Isobel and whispered in her ear, "He was talking to me earlier, and you interrupted."

Isobel turned around to Mary and said, "I didn't know. Sorry, Mary." *Yes, sorry that I am about to take Hosea away from you,* she thought as she faced the front.

The songs were sung in German, and Isobel mouthed along with the songs as if she were singing. When the singing finished, Isobel saw that a long table to the side of the room had been prepared with a large amount of food.

Isobel was not hungry, so she bypassed the food and headed to where coffee and soda were offered.

Mary was right behind her. "Is Hosea driving you home? There is a rumor that he asked you."

"I told you that already. *Jah*, he is." Isobel poured some water from a large jug into a cup before turning to face her. "He asked me, and I said yes."

"You know I like him, right? I told you that." Mary's eyes blazed through narrowed lids.

Isobel put the cup to her lips and took a mouthful of water. "Many others like him too." Isobel looked around for Hosea and saw him speaking with two young women. "Look over there now, he's speaking to them."

Mary turned to see him, and then she turned back to Isobel. "Well, obviously his sisters don't count."

When Isobel laughed at her error, Mary walked away. Isobel considered that Mary was a little snooty about things. She had never stopped Hosea from liking Mary. Clearly, he didn't like Mary, or he would've asked her on a buggy ride.

When she saw Emma again, she'd tell her that Mary wasn't a true friend.

Isobel walked a few paces from the drinks table and studied Hosea's sisters. There was no real family resemblance, and they looked roughly the same age as Hosea. One could have been older and the other younger. She wondered how many more siblings he had.

One of the sisters left Hosea and came up to her. "Emma, aren't you eating?"

"*Nee*, I had too much earlier."

"Just have one of those sugar cookies. They're the best I've ever tasted. Mary made them."

Isobel shook her head. "*Nee*, I couldn't possibly fit in

one more thing." She would have had a sugar cookie if Hosea's sister hadn't told her Mary had made them.

As time drew on, the crowd thinned out and Isobel knew that she would soon be in Hosea's buggy, and from there, she'd work her way into his heart. She smoothed down her dress, which enabled her to get rid of the sweat that was building on her palms.

Hosea looked across at her, smiled, and then walked toward her. His face was flushed, and his hair fell in loose, dark waves. "There you are. Are you ready to go?"

Isobel smiled, but she could not speak. All she could do was nod.

"Let's go." He smiled down at her as they walked out of the large barn where the singing had been held.

Once they were in his open-topped buggy, Hosea said, "It's a wondrous night."

Isobel looked up at the sky to see more bright stars than she'd ever seen in a New York sky. The moon was a large, luminous crescent that hung low in the sky. "It certainly is beautiful."

"I'll take you for a drive before I take you home."

She looked into Hosea's eyes. "I was hoping you would."

The buggy ride reminded Isobel of the horses and buggies around Central Park, which was a special treat for the tourists. Isobel considered it romantic – the two of them in a buggy under the night sky.

Isobel had come to Lancaster County to get away from Travis, not to fall in love with Hosea. She fixed her eyes on the dark road ahead wondering if she was doing something silly. Isobel did not want to lead this man on, only to leave him in a few months' time. Besides, this was the man that Emma loved. Could she really take him away from her? She knew that she could, but should she? "What are the best times you remember about us when we were younger? Do you have any nice memories?"

Hosea laughed. "There are so many. You used to come over and play with us when you were around six or seven, remember?"

Isobel nodded. *By 'us' he must mean his brothers and sisters,* Isobel thought.

"One time when we were in the fields, you and I pretended to be a married couple. You were my *fraa*. We made a little *haus* in the blackberry bushes and we had stones for chairs and a large stone for a table." Hosea threw his head back and laughed. "We had such *gut* times."

"I barely remember that," Isobel said.

"Really? Do you remember that time when your grandmother had pneumonia and you stayed with us?"

"*Jah*." Isobel nodded and hoped it had really happened and he wasn't trying to trap her, thinking she might not be Emma.

"I finally had someone younger and smaller than myself in the *haus*."

Hmm, he's the youngest and he must be quite a bit older than me if he was able to carry me around – unless he was super strong at a young age, Isobel thought. *Those two girls, his sisters, must be older than he.*

"*Jah,* we sure have had some *gut* times."

"So when did they end?" Isobel asked.

"I think we just grew apart as we got older."

"And now?" Isobel stared at his face to see how he would react to her cheeky comment.

He took his eyes off the road and fixed them upon Isobel. "And now, hopefully, we might grow closer again."

"Is that what you want?" she asked.

He looked over at her. "Yes."

Isobel believed that she saw sparks fly between them as they gazed into each other's eyes.

CHAPTER 19

*E*mma woke and as she had nothing planned, decided to take a walk around the neighborhood.

Emma took a moment to cleanse her skin and applied enough of Isobel's makeup to hide the dark circles under her eyes. She was taking a break from wearing so much makeup today. She brushed out her hair and left it down, something she'd never be able to do at home.

She pulled on a pair of jeans, ones without rips, and found them most comfortable. Lastly, she pulled on some flat lace-up shoes and a plain white T-shirt. She checked her phone again, but still no messages from Isobel. Emma made sure that she popped her phone into her bag so she could answer as soon as Isobel called.

Judging by the lack of food in Isobel's fridge, Emma figured that Isobel ate out all the time. "Well, if I'm to be Isobel that's exactly what I'll do; I'll have breakfast out, and Frank will have to pay for it." She felt a little bad, but Isobel was at home eating all her food so that balanced things out.

As Emma headed out of the apartment building, she felt good and confident to be Isobel, but she knew tomorrow would be very different. Today she would not think about the stresses of finding her way around campus; today, she would also enjoy having no chores.

Emma followed the delightful scent of coffee to a small cafe two blocks away from Isobel's apartment. Here, she felt anonymous; none of the customers looked up when she entered, not like they would have in Lancaster County.

The cafe's tables were all close together. There was a long wooden bar with stools that faced where the coffee was being made.

"What can I get you?" The young barista asked as Emma sat down at one of the tables.

"I'll have a cappuccino, please. Thank you." She smiled up at him.

He wrote it down on his order pad, then glanced up again. "Anything else?"

"Um, what's good for breakfast?" Emma looked around; no food was on show, but she could see that other people were eating.

"We've got bagels, croissants, sandwiches. We can do you a toastie…"

"Can you do a toasted sandwich with egg and cheese?"

"Sure can. Will that be on rye, white, mixed grain, gluten-free, low GI, or–"

"Just white bread thanks."

"Butter or no butter?"

"So many choices."

He smiled. "Not from around here?"

Emma shook her head. "No. I'll have butter please."

The young man nodded and turned away.

Looking around the cafe, she saw most people were either reading the newspaper or typing away on their laptops. Seeing the laptops made Emma remember to try using Isobel's when she got home. She took her phone out of her bag again to check if Isobel had tried calling – still nothing.

 Emma wished she had brought a coat with her. It seemed much colder here than at home.

The waiter brought over her food and then left just as quickly. Her first mouthful of coffee sent warmth through her whole body.

She then took a bite of her toasted sandwich and looked through the window. People were rushing by in all directions, their faces expressionless as the city bustled around them. Emma wondered where they were all headed and what their stories were. As she pondered these thoughts, her attention was suddenly drawn to a man walking past the window; he was tall, dark, and handsome, with a chiseled jawline and piercing green eyes. He looked over and caught Emma staring, and he gave her a small smile before disappearing out of sight.

 Emma felt her cheeks turn warm when she realized that he had caught her admiring him, but a jolt of excitement shot through her stomach. She finished her food quickly, grabbed her purse, and walked out of the cafe with a skip in her step. The bustling city streets filled her with an electric sense of anticipation as she set out on what promised to be a thrilling adventure.

She walked aimlessly for a while, taking in the sights and sounds —the towering skyscrapers, the honking of car horns, the chatter of people rushing by.

The sights and sounds made her wonder if Isobel was having a hard time pretending to be her, or if she was enjoying her taste of farm life.

A troubling thought jumped into her mind. If no one back home knew the difference between herself and Isobel, did anyone really know her at all?

Emma headed to a park she'd seen from the taxi when she'd first arrived.

Once she got to the park she felt more at home. The air was fresher and there were wide-open spaces. It had taken Emma longer than she thought to get to the park, so she didn't stay long before she headed back to the apartment.

As soon as she got to the street her apartment was on, she was relieved she would soon be able to rest her feet. They were aching from the unfamiliar shoes.

"Isobel."

Emma turned around to see if someone wanted to speak to her. She saw Travis not far from her.

She waited for him to come closer. "Travis, I don't think I thanked you for the other night. So, thank you."

"Don't thank me; I didn't do anything. Are you feeling better now?" He touched her shoulder gently and ran his hand down her arm.

Emma stepped back to avoid his touch. "Yes, I'm feeling much better thanks."

"Well enough to come for a walk with me?"

Emma smiled and wondered why Isobel didn't tell her what was so bad about this man. He had very good manners and he was handsome. She nodded, "Okay, but as long as we don't go too far; I've been walking all day and my feet hurt."

"Let's go up this way."

Emma's heart raced again, but not as fast as when she'd had the panic attack.

"Did you finish that essay you were working on?"

Emma did not know about any essays. "Oh, yes. I finished that one already." Emma only had an eighth-grade education like most Amish people, so she was pleased that she did not have to do any of Isobel's essays.

"That's good, but now I can't offer you any help with it."

"You would've helped me?"

"Of course, I would've."

He did not seem bad at all, nothing like Isobel had said. Isobel said that he broke her heart, but how? He was acting as if nothing had happened. Because of that, Emma was unsure how to act around him. Maybe she was too friendly given the circumstances, but she did not know what the circumstances were. She certainly could not ask him, and Isobel still hadn't called.

Travis stopped in front of a café. "Let's have a coffee here since you can't walk."

It was the first café they came to and was more of a delicatessen. "Yes, good idea."

They took seats on the sidewalk under an awning.

"I need to tell you that I'm sorry for what happened the other day," Travis said.

He did seem genuinely sorry. Emma had been taught to forgive, but Emma had to do what she thought Isobel would do. Isobel had acted devastated by what he had done and just saying sorry might not be enough for Isobel. "I was really hurt by it."

"I'll do anything to make it up to you, Isobel – anything."

Emma remained silent as she looked at the sadness on his face. What on earth would she say now?

Travis continued, "That woman you saw was nothing. You got the wrong idea, and you won't let me explain."

Emma's mouth fell open. "Other woman?" Did Travis cheat on Isobel? Now it all made sense.

Travis leaned back slightly, with his eyes fixed upon hers. "Why do you look so surprised? You're acting like it's the first time you've heard about it."

Emma stood up. "Stay away from me, Travis. Just stay away." Emma rushed away from the café, ignoring her sore feet, and didn't slow her pace until she was satisfied he wasn't following.

Within five minutes, she was home.

She sat on Isobel's couch and flipped through instructions on how to get to college and find her classrooms.

From speaking with Travis, Emma could see that she was helping Isobel by trading places with her. Isobel was undoubtedly doing the same for her and had said that she would keep an eye on Hosea.

Even though she had just met Isobel, their bond as twins was strengthening through helping each other.

CHAPTER 20

Even though she didn't have much sleep, Isobel sprang out of bed as soon as light peeked through the windows. She got changed and headed to the kitchen to make breakfast. When she got there, she found her grandmother already busy at work.

"*Mammi*," she said in surprise, "I was going to make you breakfast."

Her grandmother laughed. "I heard you moving around in your room and knew it was time for me to get up as well. I can't let you start your day before I do."

Isobel took a seat and propped her chin up with her hands.

"What happened last night with Hosea? I heard you coming home late."

Isobel tingled all over with just the mention of Hosea's name. "He's *wunderbaar*. He is the most perfect man in the world."

"*Jah*, I believe that's true, and every girl knows it," *Mammi* said.

"I'm not worried about other girls. Why? Do you think someone is going to take him away from me?"

Mammi turned her attention away from the eggs she was cooking. "You only get one chance at this, Emma. I just don't want you to miss out on him. All the girls wanted his *bruder*, Joseph, and only one girl ended up as his *fraa*."

Isobel giggled; it was as if she'd stepped back into the dark ages with women fighting over the men.

Mammi shook her head. "You won't be laughing if he turns his attention to Mary, will you?"

The smile suddenly disappeared from Isobel's face. "Mary, *nee*." Isobel screwed up her nose. "She's been horrid to me."

"She used to be your best friend until she set her sights on Hosea. I've noticed she doesn't come around so much now."

"*Jah*, I know."

Mammi spooned the eggs onto two plates, set them on the table, and sat down next to Isobel. "I've arranged a little dinner next week."

"What kind of dinner?"

"A dinner with you, me, Hosea and Hilda. At Hilda's *haus*."

"Oh, really?" Isobel knew that Hilda was Hosea's grandmother. "The two of you doing a little matchmaking, *jah*?"

Mammi laughed. "Let's just say that this is something that the two of us have wanted for some time, and now is the time to do something about it."

Isobel smiled. *"Denke."*

CHAPTER 21

By the time the special dinner at Hilda's house rolled around, Isobel had already seen Hosea twice since the buggy ride. He'd stopped by her house on two afternoons and they had strolled in the fields as the sun set. *Mammi* had been more than happy to let her off chores whenever Hosea visited, which suited Isobel just fine.

Hilda's house was small and was built onto Hosea's parents' main house.

As soon as Isobel walked in, she saw Hosea standing behind Hilda. She could feel warmth and love in the house and that love was reflected on Hilda's pleasant face.

"You have a lovely house." Isobel immediately bit her lip, as she was not sure if Amish took kindly to compliments – something about it leading to feelings of pride. Hilda did not seem to mind a compliment, though, by the look on her face.

"*Denke*, Emma. You've been here before though, haven't you?"

"*Jah*, but that was a long time ago," Isobel's grandmother said.

Hilda turned to Isobel. "You and Hosea make yourselves comfortable and Olive and I will see to dinner."

That was the first time Isobel had heard her grandmother's name. It was Olive. She'd never known that.

Hosea touched her arm. "Come sit." Hosea guided her to one of two couches, which were placed opposite each other.

Isobel was certain that she could spend all day every day with Hosea.

She sat and Hosea positioned himself next to her. He leaned in and whispered, "I think they're match-making."

Isobel tried to stop herself from giggling and whispered back, "I know for sure that they are."

"Shall we pretend to dislike each other to cause them some stress?"

Isobel put her hand to her mouth and laughed. "I don't think I could do that."

Hosea put his arm around the back of the couch behind her. "I couldn't either."

Isobel was all too familiar with the signals of love, and it was obvious to her that Hosea had strong feelings for her, if he hadn't already fallen in love. She couldn't deny the fact that she had done the same. Isobel often questioned whether the powerful emotions between them were simply a rebound from her break up with Travis. But there was something far more meaningful and intense between them than what she ever shared with Travis.

Hosea's voice disturbed her thoughts. "What do they expect us to do out here?"

"Maybe they're hoping we'll lock lips."

He burst out laughing. "The first time I kiss you, it won't be at my grandmother's house."

"Oh really? Where should it be then?" Isobel considered that it was very sweet how the Amish handled romance and relationships. However, Isobel desperately wanted him to kiss her as soon as possible.

"It will be some place special." Hosea smirked and tilted his face to the ceiling.

"When will it be? Later on tonight?" Isobel loved to tease Hosea. His eyes lit up as he laughed at Isobel.

"Lots of noise coming from out there," Hilda said.

Hosea and Isobel turned to see their two *grandmothers*, Olive and Hilda, coming back into the room with trays of food, which they set in the middle of the table.

"Smells delicious," Isobel said as she and Hosea got up and took their seats at the table.

After everyone was seated and thanks was given to *Gott* for the food, Hilda turned to Isobel. "Some of the recipes I use have been passed down through five generations of our *familye*."

"Are they secret recipes?" Isobel's eyes opened widely.

"*Jah*, most of them are secret, but of course, they won't be a secret to Hosea's *fraa* when he marries." Hilda's eyes twinkled as she peered at her friend's granddaughter.

Isobel smiled at Hilda and looked away. A moment later, Hosea and Isobel exchanged smiles. *The old ladies were way too obvious with their matchmaking.*

When dinner was finished, the two *grandmothers* suggested that Hosea and Isobel take a walk outside. Hilda had added, 'in the moonlight.'

As soon as Isobel and Hosea were outside and away from the *haus*, Hosea took hold of Isobel's hand. "It's nice to know that our families approve of us being together."

"*Jah*, I suppose that's better than not approving."

Hosea stopped and pulled Isobel toward him slightly. "I wouldn't care if they didn't approve, Emma. I wouldn't tell them that, though."

Isobel was bedazzled, as if caught in a time loop. Her life had become Emma's, and Hosea had chased away any rational thoughts she might have. All she could stammer out was, "You wouldn't be upset if they don't approve?"

"No. I have sincere emotions for you, Emma. I love you."

Isobel was dismayed. He was professing his love to Emma, but she wasn't Emma!

"Hosea," she said as she stopped walking.

"What is it, Emma?" His eyebrows scrunched together in worry as he moved to stand in front of her.

"I have something I need to say to you."

CHAPTER 22

Now that Emma had been in New York for weeks, she could say the air was polluted and the place was overcrowded. It wasn't somewhere she would go if she had a choice, but at the same time, she wasn't immune to its charms.

She had managed to find her way to and from the college and managed to find the right classrooms. Emma found some of the lectures interesting but could not understand others. She was glad that it was Isobel who was completing the essays and the assignments.

Emma had heard nothing from Isobel since she'd called asking how to milk Bessy. Emma hoped everything was okay and that her *grandmother* was well.

As Emma walked away from her last class of the day, she became aware of someone walking beside her. She looked up to see Travis.

She stopped still. "Travis."

"Will you talk with me, Isobel?" He ran a hand through his cropped hair. "I miss you."

Emma looked around to see if anyone could hear them. "You cheated on me, Travis. There's nothing to talk about."

"I didn't. I need you to hear me out."

Of course, he'd deny it. That's what cheaters did. "How do I know that you won't do it again? How can I trust you?"

"You can, Isobel. Can we talk over dinner tonight?"

Emma looked down at her feet.

"Please. If you say 'no' after tonight, then I will never bother you again, but please hear me out."

Emma looked up into his eyes and saw pain behind them and that caused her heart to soften. "Okay."

"Great." He touched her lightly on her arm, and his face relaxed into a smile. "I'll come by your place at seven."

"Okay." Emma watched Travis walk away. He seemed nice enough, but why ever would he cheat on Isobel? Surely, he couldn't have liked Isobel very much if he had gone looking for another woman. Why was Travis so insistent that he was innocent? She couldn't ask her twin because her phone was always switched off.

That night in preparation for dinner with Travis, Emma dressed how she figured that Isobel would. She wore a slinky dress and high heels. After she wore the high heels around her apartment for a little while, she could easily walk in them.

At seven o'clock, Emma walked out of her building to meet Travis.

She saw him walking toward her and couldn't help smiling. She tried not to, though, because she knew Isobel was upset with him.

Travis looked Emma up and down. "Wow, Isobel. You take my breath away."

Emma looked down at what she was wearing. "Too much? I can change."

"No, it's perfect." He smiled and then added, "You're perfect."

Travis made Emma feel special. No one ever gave her a compliment—no man did anyway. Perhaps *Mammi* had said once or twice that she'd looked nice and that was all.

Travis interrupted her daydream. "Penny for your thoughts."

Emma looked up at Travis. "What?"

"What are you thinking about?"

Emma gave a little shrug. "Oh. nothing."

"Well, are you ready?"

Emma nodded.

Travis stepped onto the road and hailed a taxi.

As Emma sat in the back of the taxi with Travis, she couldn't help but wonder how long Travis and her sister had been dating. She wished Isobel had never been interested in him so she could have met Travis under different terms. There was something about him that drew her toward him. With him, she felt safe.

Her heart suddenly raced, and she remembered what

her doctor had said, so she attempted to take long, deep breaths to avoid another panic attack.

The taxi stopped outside a restaurant. When Emma stepped onto the sidewalk, she looked up at the rustic red brick building. "This looks nice."

Travis smiled as he put his hand on the small of her back. "I remembered. It's your favorite restaurant."

Emma smiled back and nodded. 'I know."

After they were seated, the waiter handed them the menus and left them alone.

Travis looked down at the menu, and then looked up at her. "Are you having your usual?"

Emma quickly scanned the menu. "I think I'll have something different this time. The chicken Caesar salad looks good." When Travis chuckled as if she were making a joke, Emma knew that she had the same taste in food as her twin. "What will you have?"

"I'll have my usual. A thick juicy steak."

When they closed the menus, Travis looked directly into her eyes. "I need to explain what happened that day when you got so upset."

Emma put one elbow on the table. "Go on. I'm waiting to hear it."

CHAPTER 23

Travis poured them each a glass of iced water and then took a mouthful. Once he put the glass down, he began. "I know you saw me talking with another woman outside my apartment building, but you jumped to conclusions. We were honestly just talking. She's someone I knew from high school, and we'd just bumped into each other."

Emma frowned, wondering what Isobel would say. "What were you doing with her?" She'd meant to ask what they were talking about, but she didn't correct herself. Isobel was confident and she wanted to be just like Isobel. Confident people rarely corrected themselves.

Travis looked into her eyes. "We were just talking, Isobel. You don't have to be jealous. There's no other woman for me."

Emma looked off into the distance. She was sure that Isobel had said that Travis had dumped her. They must've had an argument. *Yes, that must be it. An argument about that woman.*

"Will you ever be able to forgive me?" he asked again.

Emma stared at him while wondering how best to respond. "Why do I have to forgive you if you did nothing wrong? That doesn't make sense."

"I just want things to go back to how they were before. If I have to apologize then I will."

She would forgive him, but would Isobel? And if she said 'yes' right now, then their relationship would escalate. She had to keep him at arm's length until Isobel swapped places again. "You really upset me, you know?"

"I can't stop talking to women. That would be weird."

"I don't want you to do that. It's how we argued afterward was the reason I was upset." Emma was taking a risk, but she was sure they must've argued. It was the only thing that made sense.

"I'll never argue again if you'll just give me another chance. These last weeks have been torture without you." He reached forward and grabbed hold of her hand.

Immediately, her heart beat faster, and she could feel her body tremble. She looked into his handsome face, and confusion muddled her thinking. It felt so nice to be wanted after living most of her life being unwanted by her mother. At that moment, she wanted to *be* Isobel for real. If only Hosea had spoken to her like that and been that attentive.

When Emma realized that she'd hardly thought about Hosea in weeks, she pulled her hand away.

Travis shook his head. "I'm sorry, I'm expecting too much too quickly. I know it'll take time to get back to where we were."

"That's right. I can't just turn my feelings on and off." Were her feelings for Travis overtaking the feelings she had for Hosea? Was she turning into Isobel? It seemed like it. She had to get back home as quickly as possible and get her life back. But… the only thing was Travis wouldn't be there.

"Have I upset you?" he asked.

"It's just that I'm a little dizzy." She wasn't, but she couldn't tell him the real reason she was being strange.

"Do you need anything? Can I help?"

"No. I'll be fine."

"I hope our relationship can move forward."

Emma nodded and smiled. "Like I said, I need some time, Travis. Is that okay?"

"Take all the time you want. I'm not going anywhere."

Although she felt guilty for finding her twins ex-boyfriend appealing, she knew she was doing the best thing possible for her twin. After all, Isobel was keeping all of the young women away from Hosea. She'd keep Travis 'on hold' for Isobel.

They'd swap back lives and everything would go back to normal.

CHAPTER 24

Weeks later, Emma had settled into Isobel's life and was starting to enjoy city life. Travis was a huge part of what she liked about being Isobel. Unsure of Isobel's true feelings for Travis, Emma played the cat-and-mouse game with him for as long as she could. Everything would've been much easier if Isobel had called her.

Travis was such a good man that Emma really wanted Isobel to give him another chance. She never forgot the look in Isobel's eyes as she spoke of Travis on their eighteenth birthday—she was sure that Isobel was only hurt because she was deeply in love with Travis.

The usual pattern for Emma and Travis was that they met twice a week for dinner. Travis always wanted to see her more often, but Emma had to keep things on a slow simmer.

When someone knocked on Emma's door one evening,

Emma was certain that the unexpected guest was Travis, yet a quick look through the security peephole revealed it was her mother.

Emma opened the door, and her mother walked in without saying a word.

She took off her coat and placed her expensive designer bag on a chair. "I must admit it took me a while to figure it out."

"Figure what out, Mom?"

"Don't play me for a fool."

Emma gulped. Had she found out?

"Where's Isobel?" Mom asked.

Emma closed her eyes. *She has!* Emma walked over to the couch and sat down. "How did you find out?"

Her mother moved toward her. "You're Emma?"

Emma nodded.

"I pictured this reunion quite differently." Her mother sat down as well.

Questions and feelings of rejection swirled in Emma's head. The main thing that she wanted to know from her mother was, why did she leave her and not Isobel?

They sat silently for a while before her mother said, "I guess Isobel is pretending to be you and she's with your *grandmother?*"

Emma nodded.

"And you switched some time before your birthday because that was you wasn't it, on your birthday? You were here, and Isobel was there with *Mammi?*"

Emma nodded and feelings of guilt over her deception

were so heavy within her that she could barely look at her mother. "She's still there as far as I know. We swapped on our eighteenth birthday."

"Why?"

Emma took a deep breath. "Isobel was upset and wanted a break. I guess she thought my life would be easier or something. She was upset about Travis, too. I think... mainly she was upset about Travis. They'd had some kind of argument."

"She did take it rather hard about Travis. I know she wanted to marry him. That's all she could talk about at one point."

Mom was still only concerned about Isobel, but what about her? She'd given no explanation as to why she was left with her grandmother eighteen years ago; she didn't even ask if she was happy or how her life was, or anything.

Well, if she were going to act as if nothing had happened, Emma would have to ask the questions. Emma took a deep breath. "Why did you leave me with my grandmother and take Isobel to live with you?"

Her mother shifted in her seat and licked her lips while her eyes flickered to and fro. "I'm so sorry, Emma. I know I have a lot of explaining to do. I am glad that we've met at last. I hoped for this day."

All Emma could do was stare at her and wait for an answer. She'd been waiting her whole life to hear it.

Guessing what Emma was thinking, her mother continued, "I was an unwed mother, which was not good in those days, especially not for an Amish girl. It happened when I was on *rumspringa*. Of course, I couldn't go back to the community in the position I was in."

Emma desperately wanted to interrupt and ask about her father, but she decided to let her finish what she had to say.

"I found out that I was having twins. I already had a job as a nanny with a couple with two older children and a baby. They said that they would let me keep working for them, but they only had room for one baby. Of course, they were an *Englisher* couple." She cleared her throat. "Can I have some water?"

"Sure." Emma poured a glass of water, handed it to her mother and quickly sat back down.

After a few sips of water, her mother continued, "I could have gone back to the Amish, I suppose, and lived with the shame after I publicly confessed my sin, but I couldn't bring continual shame on my mother. So I decided to keep the job and keep one baby. The other baby —you— I left with my mother. I was in a bad position. I had no other choice. My mother had no money to help me out. I had nowhere to turn. In those days, there weren't the options that there are today."

"How did you choose?" Emma knew her tone was harsh; she was angry and did not care if it showed.

"Choose what?"

"Why did you take Isobel and leave me with *Mammi*? It's something I've wanted to know for years."

CHAPTER 25

"I didn't really choose either baby. I took a taxi with both twins to your grandmother's house from the hospital and just handed her the nearest baby. That was you."

"Are you saying that I ended up being brought up Amish because I was the closest baby to the door? That changed the course of my life. I thought you would've had a reason at least. Or that you would've struggled with the decision."

Her mother wiped away a tear. "It was the hardest thing that I ever had to do. There was no way to choose. The truth is, I opened the car door and handed one baby to my mother."

Emma grunted. "I don't believe it was a hard decision. I'm sorry, but I don't. You never visited, never wrote – nothing. Nothing at all. Not even a birthday card."

Her mother stared into her eyes. "It was too hard, Emma. It was too hard for me. I didn't want to disrupt the life that you had. I knew you would have a good life with my mother as I had. I didn't want to confuse you. It was the easiest thing for both of us if we kept apart."

Emma crossed her arms over her chest. "I've always felt that you didn't want me, and I was left to wonder why you took my twin instead of me. I always thought that I wasn't good enough for you." It hurt Emma even to say the words.

Emma's mother put her hands up to her face and cried. Emma thought she should put her arm around her and comfort her, but she couldn't find any compassion inside of her.

Emma got up to fetch her some tissues. Then she handed them to her mother and watched her dry her tears.

"Eighteen years, eighteen years with no word, no word at all." Emma could not stop from saying words she knew would hurt, but she had to get them out. "I grew up as an only child, but I wasn't. I had a sister. I had a twin. How could you break apart twins? Twins belong with each other. They have twin hearts, twin souls. They are two halves of a whole."

"I'm sorry. I'm really sorry. I wish I could take it back and find another way. There are so many decisions I would change if I could."

Emma pressed her lips tightly together and stared at the woman in front of her. She was little more than a stranger. In Emma's eyes, it was too late for her mother to cry about it now – much too late.

"Do you think that we could be friends?" Her mother spoke through her tears.

Emma nodded and fixed a smile on her face. She could try to be friends. After all, she was her twin's mother, but she could never love this woman as a mother. Not after she had no contact with the selfish woman for eighteen years.

"So does Frank know that Isobel and I traded places?" Emma asked.

Her mother nodded. "Yes, Frank and I tell each other everything."

Emma tried to stop her fingers from fidgeting. "How long have you been with him?"

"Nearly ten years now."

"Ten years, and you've not married?" Emma screwed up her face.

"We've talked of marriage, but that's as far as things have gotten."

"Hmm, I see." Emma did not approve of living together; it was clear that her mother had not taken the Amish values with her when she left the community. The woman did as she wished and only cared about herself, that was plain to see. "Are you going to call *Mammi* and tell her what Isobel and I did?"

"No. It'll do Isobel good to live amongst the Amish for a while, and in some way it might be helpful to live in each other's shoes for a while." Mom sniffled. "I'm sorry you were raised as an only child. Was that tough?"

"It was, but I had a lot of friends and that helped. There were always other children around." Emma's mind drifted to a time when her grandmother was very ill, and there was no sign of her mother then. "When was the last time you spoke to *Mammi*?"

"It's been a while. We had a bit of a falling out and haven't spoken for years."

"What did you fall out over?" Emma did not usually ask this many questions, but she figured that she was entitled to know a few things.

Her mother sniffed a couple more times before she said, "Over you, actually."

Emma tucked her legs underneath her. "What about me?"

"A few years back, she said that I should come to see you. I said no. I was scared of how you would be toward me."

Emma shook her head, as she was lost for words. She tried not to judge her mother and steered the conversation to her twin. "How long has Isobel known that she had a twin?"

"Just a few short years. Growing up, she was always asking for a sister. It's as if she knew that she should have had one." Mom wiped away another tear.

"Don't cry. Shall I call Frank?"

Her mother put up her hand. "No, I'll be all right in a minute."

"I don't like to see you upset like this." Even though she was mad at her mother, she never liked to see anyone upset.

"I guess I knew that this day would come, and I just knew that you'd be angry that I left you. I would never leave you with anyone else but my mother. I knew I was putting you in the best possible hands. If I couldn't raise you, the best person to do it was your grandmother."

Emma remained silent. She'd had a good life growing up in the community, but there were always the unanswered questions and there was always the other life that she could have had – if only. If only Isobel had been the one closest to the door of the taxi when her mother left a baby with *Mammi*.

"I guess I was looking for a reason why you left me. I wasn't expecting that you would say that I was the closest one to the door." Emma thought that her words might have hurt her mother, but at that point, it had become about her, not about someone else. Emma had always been concerned for other people and how they were feeling, but now she decided to be concerned about herself and how she felt.

"I know it must sound silly to you, but there was no way to make a choice. How do you choose between two people you love the most in the world? I loved you and Isobel equally. There was no difference between the two of you. You were both such delightful babies."

"How long was I with you before…"

"Five days. I'm sorry that I failed you as a mother."

Emma grunted. "Don't be sorry."

Her mother dabbed her eyes with a tissue and sniffed a couple more times. "I will try to make it up to you, Emma."

"It's fine, really. I've had a good life with *Mammi*. There's no need to make it up." But deep down, Emma knew that she wanted more from her mother than just a casual friendship. She wanted the connection that only a mother and daughter could have. Emma had always felt a void in her life, a longing for something she could never quite grasp. And now, facing her mother after all these years, that void had only grown larger.

As Emma sat there, lost in thought, her mother spoke up. "You know, there's something I've been wanting to give you for a long time." She reached into her purse and pulled out a small envelope. "It's a letter I wrote to you when you were born. I never got the chance to give it to you, but I've held onto it all these years."

Emma took the envelope and opened it slowly. Inside was a handwritten letter dated the day she was born.

As she read the words, tears streamed down her face. Her mother had written about her hopes and dreams for Emma, about the love she had for her and her twin, and about the impossible decision she had to make.

Emma looked up at her mother, her eyes still glistening with tears. "Thank you," she whispered.

Her mother gave her a sad smile. "I know it can't make up for everything, but maybe it can help you understand why I did what I did."

Emma nodded, tucking the letter into her pocket. She wasn't sure if she could forgive her mother yet, but the letter had softened her heart. She'd hold onto that letter as a keepsake.

As they sat there in silence, Emma's mind raced with all the questions she wanted to ask.

CHAPTER 26

As more weeks rolled by, Emma was increasingly concerned that there was no contact whatsoever with Isobel. She had no idea what was happening. She'd only wanted to be gone for a week and Isobel had talked her into staying longer. Emma could not plan for anything in her life if she didn't know when they were swapping back lives.

It was late October when Emma's mother knocked on the door of Isobel's apartment.

Emma opened the door. "Mom. What's wrong? You look as white as a sheet."

She hurried to the couch and sat down to catch her breath. "I got a phone call from your grandmother earlier today."

Emma clutched at her throat. "Is she all right?"

"Yes, she's fine. She called to tell me Isobel is getting married later today."

Emma gasped. "What?"

"Yes. As crazy as it sounds apparently it's true."

"Getting married to an Amish *man?* Or has she left the community?"

"An Amish man. Isobel told *Mammi* that she didn't want either of us to know, but *Mammi* thought we should. She called me without Isobel knowing. *Mammi* also knows that you two traded places. I'm not sure when she found that out."

Emma felt a sharp pain in her heart as though a dagger had been driven through it. Why would Isobel not want her to know, and why was she getting married so quickly? "Who is she marrying, Mom?"

"I can't remember. It was an unusual name."

"It wasn't Hosea, was it?" Emma shut her eyes tightly and waited for her mother's answer.

"Yes, that's it, Hosea. I've hardly heard that name. I know it's from the Bible, but you don't …" Emma's mother noticed that Emma had fallen to the floor. She raced over to her, and Emma reached up and grabbed her mother's hand.

"How long will it take us to get there if we leave now?" Emma was so weak from shock; she could hardly speak.

"I'd say two and a half, maybe three hours."

"Did you drive here?" Emma asked.

Her mom nodded.

Emma pulled herself to her feet. "Hurry, we have to get there and stop them. I'm supposed to marry Hosea."

"You were going to marry him?"

"Yes. This is all wrong."

"I totally agree. Isobel has taken this swap too far."

CHAPTER 27

When Emma and her mother were half an hour into their trip, Emma's cell phone rang. It was Travis. In all the fuss she forgot that Travis would be devastated that Isobel would be marrying another. It was partly her fault for leading him on and having him believe he might have a chance with Isobel.

She took a deep breath and answered the phone.

"Isobel, where are you? Did you forget I was coming over?"

"I don't know how to explain this to you. There's so much you don't know about things."

"Where are you? It sounds like you're in a car."

"I'm not Isobel. I'm Emma, Isobel's twin. Our mother gave me away at birth and kept Isobel. I'm from an Amish community, and the man I was to marry is now going to marry someone else who he thinks is me, and I must stop him."

"You were going to marry someone? Wait, if you're not Isobel, can I speak with her?" he asked.

"Put him on loudspeaker," Emma's mother said.

Emma switched him over to the loudspeaker and closed her eyes.

"Hello Travis, it's Isobel's Mom. You knew Isobel was a twin, didn't you?"

"She mentioned it. Can you tell me what's going on?"

"Isobel and her twin, Emma, swapped places and have been living as each other for months. Now Isobel is about to marry the man Emma was supposed to marry. He thinks she's Emma and it seems Isobel is going along with it. She must've lost her mind completely."

There was silence from Travis' end of the phone.

"You still there, Travis?" Emma's mom asked.

"So for the last few months, I've been seeing Emma and not Isobel?"

"That's right. I'm sorry, Travis. I don't know what to say. I'm sorry you got caught up in all this."

"I'm coming too. I'll meet you there."

"No, Travis," Emma said.

"We've already left," Mom said.

Then their phone connection was lost.

∼

EMMA MADE her mother drive as quickly as she could without stopping. Emma knew the wedding would be taking place at her house.

Emma wondered why *Mammi* was going along with the wedding if she knew they had traded places. That led her to think about what had motivated Isobel to swap with her in the first place. "Isobel told me that you taught her Pennsylvania Dutch when she was young. Weren't you afraid she'd wonder why you were doing that?"

"No. She knew I grew up Amish."

"Oh, that's right. I'm doubting everything she told me."

"I wouldn't say I taught her. I might've told her a couple of words. If she knows it, she could've learned it from anywhere."

"She said you taught her. She'd have to know it so she could fool people into thinking she was me. I have to wonder how long she had this planned."

"Isobel has a reason behind everything she does. I'd say she would've been plotting it for some time."

Emma thought back to the notebook Isobel had given her. "She gave me a thick notebook all about her life. That would've taken her some time to do."

"Honestly, Emma, sometimes I feel I don't know Isobel at all. I certainly don't know what goes on in her mind."

"It seems that makes two of us even though she is my twin."

As soon as they rounded the corner from one of the main roads, the old farmhouse came into view. There were what seemed like hundreds of buggies outside the house.

The car zoomed to the front door, then Emma jumped

out and ran into the house. "Stop, stop this whole thing," Emma yelled.

Isobel and Hosea were standing before the bishop and they both swung around to look at Emma, as did everyone else in the room.

The bishop gazed from Isobel to Emma, and back again. "What's going on?" he asked.

Emma ran to Hosea. "Hosea, she's not me. She's my twin. I'm the real Emma."

Hosea looked from Emma to Isobel.

CHAPTER 28

Hosea took a deep breath as he stared at Emma. "I know, Emma. Isobel told me the whole thing."

The bishop stepped forward and said to her, "You didn't know about this, Emma?"

Emma ran away without answering the bishop, and Hosea ran after her. "Wait, Emma."

When Emma was out of earshot of the wedding guests, she turned around and waited for Hosea to catch up with her.

Hosea stood in front of her. "What's got you so upset, Emma?"

"Don't you understand? That's not me. That's my twin. She's Isobel. The woman you were about to marry is Isobel. *I'm Emma!*"

Hosea scratched his head. "I fell in love with Isobel the first day she arrived here, on your eighteenth birthday. At first, I didn't know it wasn't you, but I fell in love with her on that very day. I know she's Isobel."

Emma pouted. "That's the day she made me swap with her."

"I know. I've always liked you, Emma, but with Isobel it's different. It's like something that I can't even describe to you."

Tears ran down Emma's face and she could not stop them. "But she's not really Amish; she's an *Englisher*."

"Was, Emma. Isobel was an *Englisher*. She's been baptized now, she's taken the instructions, so she is Amish and we're getting married."

"You know nothing of her. Nothing about her, at all. I've found out some horrible things about her." She leaned in close to Hosea and wiped her tears with the back of her hand. "She's really not a nice person."

"That's all in the past."

Emma shook her head. She'd lived a *good* life and done everything right, and now her sinful sister with a sordid past was about to marry the man she loved. How was it fair?

Hosea put his hand gently on her shoulder. "Didn't you get the letter?"

"What letter?"

"Isobel sent you a letter explaining everything and telling you we're getting married."

"I never got a letter. You see – she's a liar as well. Isobel told *Mammi* not to tell us. We weren't to know. The only reason we knew to come here is that *Mammi* called my mother."

Hosea looked down and scraped his foot on the ground. "Emma, I can't listen to you say these things about Isobel. We're getting married, and I'd like you to be happy for us."

Isobel approached them and called from a distance. "Hosea, is everything all right?"

Hosea called over his shoulder. "I'll be there in a minute."

At this point, Emma knew it was no use telling Hosea about Isobel's faults. He didn't want to hear it. Still, she could not stop herself. "She can't even speak to me because she knows she's done wrong by me, forcing me to leave here. She can't even look at me."

"Will you come back and watch us be married and be happy for us?'

"*Nee*, I can't. If you go through with this, you're making a big mistake. Can't you see that?" Emma grabbed Hosea's arm. "She's very persuasive. She made me go to New York to pretend to be her – I didn't even want to, but somehow, she made me do it. Now she's making you marry her. She's conniving, convincing, and coercive."

Hosea took hold of Emma's arm and placed it down by her side, and said, "I need to go back and get married. Will you come and watch, please? It'll mean a lot to Isobel."

"Emma."

Emma looked over Hosea's shoulder to see her mother.

Her mother beckoned to her to come toward her. "You're making a scene and embarrassing yourself."

Emma looked into Hosea's eyes and saw that it was no use. He had made up his mind to marry Isobel, or rather he had been manipulated into marrying Isobel. At this point, it was useless. Once again, Isobel was preferred over her. It was the ongoing story of her life.

"I'll not watch this." Emma turned and walked away, unheard and feeling like a fool. Hosea had never loved her. Not only that, she'd embarrassed herself in front of her whole community.

Emma had never felt more alone in her life.

CHAPTER 29

Once Hosea returned to stand with Isobel, the bishop resumed speaking. Before the interruption, the service had been nearly finished. The bishop had already counseled Isobel and Hosea privately that they might be moving too fast with the marriage. After all, Isobel had only just been baptized and had not been raised within their faith. Hosea and Isobel had managed to convince the bishop that they were more than ready to be married. He had reluctantly agreed with their decision.

After being legally wed, Isobel looked into Hosea's eyes and felt a surge of exhilaration. She had imagined herself getting married but never to an Amish man. She thought back to when she'd taken Emma's place and promised to watch over Hosea and keep Mary from him. Isobel glanced around but didn't see Emma anywhere, just the stoic Mary in the front row staring at her with contempt.

Isobel had been reluctant to invite her mother and

CHAPTER 29

twin sister Emma to her wedding since she thought one of them might cause a scene. As it happened, Emma did, and that justified her keeping them away.

Now that she and Hosea were a married couple, Isobel wondered if her twin could ever forgive her for keeping the knowledge of the wedding quiet.

One day, she hoped she and Emma would be close, as twins should be. She was aware that Emma still held a torch for Hosea, but there was nothing she could do when Hosea's heart belonged only to her.

One thing Isobel was sure of was that she had the most wonderful, handsome man in the world. Not only that, she had learned about *Gott* as well.

∼

Emma stood away from the house that she had grown up in, where her twin was getting married to the man she loved.

Everyone she knew had betrayed her.

The worst thing was that she could not live with her grandmother now, not now that she had condoned Isobel's behavior.

Mammi had known about them trading places before Isobel's baptism. She must have seen a relationship developing between Isobel and Hosea and yet did nothing to stop it.

Mammi had Mom's number. She could've called to get a message to her, but she hadn't bothered until it was far too late.

Emma let out a large sigh and sat on a tree stump near the barn. She had nowhere to go and no one to turn to. Even *Gott* had deserted her since He allowed the marriage of Isobel and Hosea to take place.

A wave of nausea overtook her as it hit her that marriage was something that could not be revoked – not amongst the Amish.

Why Gott, why? Am I being punished for deceiving people into thinking that I was Isobel? Surely a punishment such as this is too harsh for such a sin.

Emma stood up and was about to go into the fields where she could cry alone, and then her attention was drawn to a fast-traveling car coming toward the house. She squinted and saw the car looked much like Travis' car.

When the vehicle turned into the driveway, tears fell down her cheeks. He pulled the car over and parked it behind the buggies. Emma ran to him. "It's too late. They're married now."

"You are?"

"What do you mean? Oh. I'm Emma." Now she felt even more alone. "I've been pretending to be Isobel for the last six months." She pointed to the house. "Isobel is in there, but she's married now. It's too late to stop it. I deceived you and I'm so sorry." She wiped her eyes. "I was keeping Isobel's place until she returned, and now it seems she's never going to return because she just married Hosea. I was supposed to marry him."

"I'm so sorry, Emma. Were you engaged to Hosea?"

CHAPTER 29

"No, but... No. I'm glad you're here, Travis. I know you're upset about this too."

"I'll survive."

Emma burst into tears, and Travis put his arms around her.

Now that Emma had been betrayed by the people closest to her, she didn't know where she would go, or what she would do. All she knew for certain was that Travis would always be a close friend, even though he was an *Englisher*.

CHAPTER 30

"Where's your mother?" Travis asked.

"I'm not sure. I think she's talking in the house with Isobel. I hope Mom comes out here soon so we can go home."

Thoughts swirled through Emma's mind. Where would she live, and how would she support herself now that she could not return to the community?

Out of the corner of her eye, she saw movement outside the house. *Mammi* was hurrying toward her.

Travis saw her as well. "Looks like someone wants to speak with you."

"It's my grandmother."

"I'll leave you two to talk."

Emma could barely speak as her grandmother extended her arms toward her. It had been nearly six months since she'd seen her, and she'd missed her terribly.

CHAPTER 30

"Emma, I'm so sorry. Isobel said she wrote you a letter explaining everything. I thought it was strange when I heard nothing from you, so I phoned your *mudder*."

"I know, *denke*." Her grandmother's arms usually held comfort, but nothing could comfort her today. Emma drew back a little. "There was no letter, *Mammi*. If you hadn't called Mom, we wouldn't even have known."

Her grandmother shook her head as though she was disappointed in Isobel. "Two days ago, I asked Isobel why I hadn't heard from you, and she just brushed my question aside. I should've done something about it then." Her grandmother pressed her thin lips together and shook her head. "That was when I figured that she hadn't sent a letter."

At least her grandmother hadn't betrayed her. "So when did you realize that Isobel wasn't me?"

Mammi's blue eyes peered into Emma's. "Swapping places with her was a silly thing to do."

She was right, of course, but it hurt Emma to hear it.

"Isobel confessed everything and then said she wanted to take the instructions and get baptized. I knew it was because she was in love with Hosea and him with her. Before that, I did think you – I mean she, pretending she was you, had gone a little daft, not remembering things, but I figured you to be in love. It all made sense when Isobel told me who she really was."

Emma put her head in her hands and sobbed.

Mammi stroked Emma's back. "Don't cry. It wasn't

CHAPTER 30

meant to be. *Gott* will have someone more suited to you; just you wait and see."

Travis walked back to Emma when he saw her distressed. "Are you all right, Emma?"

Emma looked up and forced a smile, "I'm fine. Travis, this is my grandmother."

"Nice to meet you, Travis. I'm Olive Byler."

"Nice to meet you as well, Mrs. Byler."

Her grandmother had a twinkle in her eye when she looked up at the handsome Travis. She turned to Emma. "Who is to know the mind of *Gott*?"

Emma wanted to shout. She wanted to say out loud that *Gott* had abandoned her for deceiving people, but if that were true, why wasn't Isobel being punished as well?

Everything always goes Isobel's way; it's clear Gott is blessing Isobel and punishing me. Mom chose Isobel instead of me, and now Hosea has chosen Isobel over me.

Her grandmother folded her arms. "Don't look so distressed. All this must be for a good reason, child."

Emma could not figure out any reason for the only man she ever loved to marry someone else. "Oh, this is so terrible; everything is so wrong. I'm having a bad dream. Is that it, is it a dream?"

"It's okay, Emma." Travis stepped close and put an arm around her shoulder.

Her grandmother lowered her voice. "There's something else that you won't be pleased about, but I must tell you."

CHAPTER 30

Emma's head shot up to look at her *Mammi's* face. "It gets worse? What is it?"

"Hosea and Isobel will be living with me until they can buy a house of their own."

Emma shook her head. "That does it. She's taken over my life completely." She'd lost her place completely.

"Don't worry. You can live here too," *Mammi* told her. "There is plenty of room."

"I can't ever live around here again. Didn't you see me burst into the house and try to stop the wedding?"

Mammi's gaze fell to the ground as Emma continued ranting,

"I shall never forget that, not in a gazillion years. I feel like such a fool." Emma threw her hands up in the air. "I am a fool. A complete and utter idiot." Defeated, Emma hurried away to be by herself.

Isobel had taken over her life so did she have to take over Isobel's life? And if she didn't want to do that, what would she do?

All her life she assumed she'd marry a man from the community, make a home, and have babies, but now that wasn't an option.

Emma sat on a pile of fence palings facing the house. As she looked up, she saw her mother striding toward her.

Emma stood up. "I can't live here with them. Of course, I can't." Emma held her head, which was throbbing.

"Move in with Frank and me. I'd love it if you did that.

CHAPTER 30

Then you wouldn't be alone. We could have a lot of fun together. We can get our nails done, go shopping, and do all the things we never got to do. We'll make up for lost time."

Emma pressed her lips together. Frank never showed that he even liked her very much, but she had gotten closer to her mother over the last few weeks.

"The only other option is to live in Isobel's apartment, but that's Isobel's place, and I'm not Isobel – not anymore." Emma shook her head. "I don't know how my own twin could do this to me."

Her mother lifted Emma's chin with one finger. "Well, it's done, and you'll have to get over it. All's fair in love and war, as they say."

Mammi joined them. "I'm sorry, Emma. I must get back and help with the food. I'm the organizer today. Are you staying around?"

"Nee, I'll be going soon." Emma hugged her grandmother goodbye.

"Write to me, Emma. You're welcome to come home anytime you wish. I've missed you so much."

"I've missed you too, *Mammi.*" Of course, her grandmother had to go and tend to Isobel's wedding while Emma's heart was breaking. As she watched her grandmother hurry back to the house, Emma wondered why Isobel was always more important.

Emma bit her tongue as she thought everything through. Isobel was the chosen child. Isobel did not even deserve to have a wedding. She certainly did not deserve

CHAPTER 30

to live in her grandmother's house, and she didn't deserve Hosea!

Why did Isobel get everything?

"I don't know how Hosea has been fooled into loving her." Emma was not even aware that she had spoken out aloud.

Her mother put her hands firmly on Emma's shoulders. "Now, cut out this nonsense. I heard what Hosea said. He knew full well he was marrying Isobel and not you. You can't force someone to love you. He had a choice, and he chose Isobel. It might hurt now, but you will get over it in time and you'll be better off for it."

Travis walked back over to her. "Is there anything I can do?"

Emma looked up into Travis' kind face. "You've had a shock too, Travis. I know how you feel about her."

"I'll survive and so will you. We can get through it together." He gave Emma a reassuring smile.

All Emma wanted to do was go—leave Lancaster County and the Amish behind her. She would have to start a new life; she was forced to start a new life because hers had been stolen by her twin.

Emma bit her bottom lip again and stared at the house she grew up in. If only she hadn't answered the door on her eighteenth birthday when Isobel had knocked on it. If only she had said 'no' to the ridiculous idea of trading places. If only she hadn't been so eager to please her twin.

Her mother interrupted her thoughts. "Come and live with Frank and me. You can go back to Isobel's apartment

CHAPTER 30

and use it for as long as you want, but as I said, I think you need to be around people who love you, not by yourself. What do you say?"

Emma had only been to her mother's house a few times over the past months. "Thanks, Mom. I'd like that, but only for a while until I decide what I'm going to do."

"Good," her mother said. "We can make up for lost time."

Resentment resurfaced in Emma when she thought about sitting in those classes posing as Isobel for all those months. It was all for nothing. Emma knew that bitterness was a bad thing, but she couldn't help it.

"I'm heading back now. What about you two?" Travis asked.

"Yes, I think we should go. Can we get out of here, Mom?"

"Sure we can. I'll just say goodbye to Isobel and—what was his name again?" Mom asked.

"Hosea." It pained Emma to say his name.

"That's right, Hosea. I won't be a moment." Her mother handed Emma the car keys. "You go wait in the car. I won't be long. Or, do you want to travel back with Travis?"

"Mom. I'm being selfish. You should stay; it's your daughter's wedding." She glanced up at Travis.

"Yes, Rose, you should stay. I'll book us rooms in town somewhere for the night and text you the details."

Rose shook her head. "Isobel didn't want me here. Did you forget that?"

CHAPTER 30

From the look on her mother's face, Emma could see she was hurt and angry by the way they had both been treated by Isobel. "I guess I did. I'll travel back with you, Mom."

Her mother nodded toward her dark green BMW. "You go to the car, and I'll be back in a minute, and then we can leave."

After her mother was nearly at the house, Emma turned toward Travis. "I'm sorry. I would've gone back with you, only Mom's upset."

"That's fine, Emma. I'll head back now, then, if you're certain you're okay."

"I'll be fine. They say time heals all wounds. I'll find out if that's true."

"Same here. I'll see you soon." He walked away.

"Thank you for being concerned about me, Travis."

He gave her a beaming smile. "Always. Let's meet up tomorrow night and we can debrief all this."

"I'd love that." She watched him walk to his car, and when he turned around, smiled, and gave her a little wave, her worries were temporarily gone.

After Travis left, Emma looked down at the keys in her hand. The smell of hot roast meats wafted under her nose. She breathed the aroma deeply while scenes of past weddings and special community events rolled through her mind. She'd always had such a good time at them. At every wedding, she'd imagine what her own would be like. Now, none of it was going to happen. There was only one person to blame!

CHAPTER 30

Emma walked toward the car, pleased that her mother was just as anxious to get away from the place as she was.

Emma clicked the car's remote to unlock the doors. She sank into the leather seats and closed her eyes. When she opened them, she tried to see what was going on, but she was too far away to see anything.

As Emma inhaled the fumes of new-car leather, she tried to talk herself into feeling better. She had a chance to reinvent herself and be anyone that she wanted.

Emma's positive self-talk was extremely short-lived because when it came to identity, the only way she could know who she was, was to know where she'd come from. She knew who her mother was, but what about her father?

Now more than ever, it was important to find out who he was. She wondered if her mother knew where to find him, and if so, would she tell her?

Emma's stomach clenched when she realized she would most likely have to find out by other means, considering the way her mother kept secrets.

Emma shrugged at the images of her embarrassment of stopping Hosea and Isobel's wedding.

The incident would be gossip-fodder for the community members for years to come.

CHAPTER 31

Back at the house, Isobel turned to Hosea. "I should talk with Emma."

"Nonsense, it's our wedding day. I've spoken to her. She'll be fine. Put her out of your mind." Hosea took hold of Isobel's hand and repeated, "She'll be fine."

Isobel nodded. "Okay. What did you say to Emma?" Isobel asked.

"I explained that it's you I love and that I fell in love with you on your birthday—the day that the both of you traded places."

Isobel licked her lips. She had hoped Emma would find out about their marriage long after the wedding. It was embarrassing now that everyone knew she'd deliberately been keeping things a secret from Emma and her mother. Most of all, she didn't want her husband to think she was anything less than a perfect wife. "What did she say to that?"

CHAPTER 31

He simply said, "She understood."

Isobel tugged on Hosea's arm. "But I think she's really upset. What if she never speaks to me again?"

"That's a bridge that we'll cross when we come to it. Besides, it's a little late now to consider her feelings."

Her jaw dropped open. Her new husband did think she was awful.

Hosea pulled her hand to his mouth and gave it a quick kiss. "It's our wedding. We must remember this day as joyful."

"Just let me go and talk to Emma, and then I can concentrate on enjoying myself."

Hosea gently guided Isobel to the window. "Look out there. She's already gone. I can't see her anywhere, and I'll not have you running around outside on our wedding day trying to explain yourself to someone who's upset."

"But she's my twin."

"She'll be fine." Hosea held her hand a little tighter. "Now come with me, Mrs. Schrock."

Isobel's whole body tingled at the sound of being called Mrs. Schrock. She was now Hosea's wife, and no other woman could ever steal him away – not Mary, not Emma, and not anyone.

Hosea led her by the arm to the corner of the room where they were setting up the wedding table. There were hundreds of guests, so some tables were being set up outside the house as well. Isobel was now a proper Amish woman, and she couldn't be happier.

Now she was making up for the loneliness she had

experienced as a child. She not only had Hosea and *Mammi*, but she also had a whole community she could call her family. She only wished marrying Hosea had not come at the price of her sister's happiness. She knew Emma was furious with her. It was the only blot in her perfect life.

Isobel knew she'd have to come up with a good excuse for not telling them about the wedding. She decided to say that she had intended to call Emma and her mother before the wedding, but everything happened so fast that she simply ran out of time.

It was months ago that Isobel had told everyone in the community who she really was, that she had deceived them, and that she was really Isobel, Emma's twin sister—an *Englischer*.

The bishop had accepted her confession and granted her permission to take the instructions and to be baptized. It helped that Isobel had lived the Amish lifestyle a little prior to her baptism. Of course, Isobel had given the bishop the impression that Emma knew everything that was going on.

Would the bishop punish her in some way? Would she have to stand up and make a public confession–again?

Isobel distracted herself from the rude interruption to the wedding with the fact that she had made sure that Mary was sitting next to one of Hosea's older brothers, Caleb. Caleb was the second oldest son of the Schrocks and had never married. Isobel thought that Mary and Caleb might make a good pair.

CHAPTER 31

Mary and Isobel had become friends even though Mary was one of the girls who desired to be Hosea's wife. To make amends, Isobel thought it a good idea to match her with someone else, and who better than Hosea's older brother?

Moments after Isobel had taken her seat at the wedding table, she saw her mother hurrying toward her. "Isobel, I just want to say congratulations to you, and you too, Hosea." She smiled at them both, and Hosea stood up and extended his hand. Her mom kissed Hosea on both cheeks and then leaned down and kissed Isobel.

"You'll stay, won't you, Mom?"

"No, I've got Emma in the car. I told her I'd drive her back."

"She's not staying?"

"No. You know she's not. *Mammi* called me and told me about the wedding this morning." Her mother looked from Isobel to Hosea and then back to Isobel.

Isobel could see the disappointment in her mother's eyes; she could also feel the disappointment coming from Hosea.

"I guess that means you'll be staying here, in the community?" her mother asked.

"*Jah*, I will." It seemed to Isobel that on the most important day of her life, her wedding day, everyone was disappointed in her—Hosea, her mom, her twin, and also her grandmother. Isobel closed her eyes. *This is not how it's supposed to be. Everyone is supposed to be happy for me.* Isobel opened her eyes to see her mother looking at her intently.

CHAPTER 31

Isobel stammered, "I - I'm glad you came. Sorry about everything. I'll write to you."

"Yes, do that. I might come and visit soon with Frank."

There was tension in the air that Isobel tried to ease by saying, "I was going to tell you, Mom. I was going to tell you and Emma, but I just... I just ran out of time." It didn't sound as convincing as it had been when she'd rehearsed it in her head moments before.

Her mother nodded, turned around, and walked away.

Isobel watched her mother walk to the kitchen. Isobel guessed she was going to say goodbye to her grandmother before she left.

Now she could write to her friends and tell them what had happened. Isobel knew that they would never understand. They would never understand that she had given up all the modern conveniences of the world and stepped back two hundred years in time to live amongst the Amish. But this is the life she chose, and she loved it.

CHAPTER 32

In what seemed to Emma like an eternity later, her mother returned to the car.

Highly embarrassed, Emma sat slumped low in the car, wondering what they were saying about her. Even her friends, Mary Miller, Katie and Lizzy Lapp, hadn't come out to talk with her. That said a lot.

"I can't wait to get away from this place."

Her mother did not say anything when she got into the car, she just started the engine and drove away.

Half an hour later, her mother glanced sideways at her. "You're very quiet, Emma."

"I'm still in shock. I've just spent the last few months pretending to be Isobel, and now I find out that I can't even go back to my own home. I was doing her a favor all these months and all the while…" Emma's voice trailed away. She swallowed hard and knew there was no use going on about it.

CHAPTER 32

"I know. It's awful for you, but Frank and I are here for you."

After a moment, Emma said, "I'm thinking about what to do. I'll have to get a job or something. I don't know how to do anything." All she had done for the past months was pretend to be Isobel, go to her classes, and live on Frank's money. She couldn't do that now.

Her mother glanced in her direction again. "*Mammi* taught you how to sew, didn't she?"

"*Jah*, we sewed together quite a lot in the evenings." A smile came to Emma's face as she remembered the nights she spent with *Mammi* talking and quilting while they drank meadow tea and ate sugar cookies.

"You could make quilts. Amish quilts sell for a lot of money. You'd most likely be surprised what they sell for."

Emma scoffed. "That's an Amish thing to do. I don't feel as though I'm Amish anymore, so I don't want to do something like that." She knew she had to find some way to make money. She didn't want to be a burden on anyone.

"Why don't you go back to school?"

"No. I don't like school, not since I've had to sit in college every day for the past few months. No." Emma crossed her arms over her chest and shook her head. "You know what? I was thinking about it before. I think Isobel didn't even do any of her college work at all. I've just wasted months of my life." When her mother made no comment, she added, "I'd say, as soon as she met Hosea, she forgot all about college."

"You might be right, but don't upset yourself about

CHAPTER 32

things like that now. You can't change the past, but you do have to think about your future. You don't have to make up your mind straight away. Just have a rest and get over the shock of everything."

Emma muttered, "Okay." If only Isobel could feel the pain that she was going through right now, how would she like it if the tables had been turned?

∼

Mary Miller was the last guest to leave the wedding. Isobel followed her to the door, kissed her goodbye, and watched her walk to her buggy in the dark. As Isobel closed the front door, she heard a clattering sound coming from the kitchen.

Although quite a few people had stayed back to help clean the place, it was still in need of more cleaning. Isobel walked into the kitchen and saw that *Mammi* was bending over the stove, mopping up some food spills. "You go to bed now, *Mammi*. Hosea and I will clean up."

Mammi stood up and said, *"Nee,* I'll just do a little bit, so there's less to do in the morning."

Hosea walked into the kitchen, and both women looked up at him. *"Nee,* Olive, please go to bed now. Isobel and I will fix this."

Olive put the scouring pad down on the sink. "Well, if you're sure. I'm rather tired, and my old bones could do with a lie down."

CHAPTER 32

"*Jah*, we're sure," Hosea said with a laugh in his voice. "Off you go."

Mammi smiled at the two of them, wiped her hands on a dishtowel, and left Hosea and Isobel alone in the kitchen.

"Hosea, look at all this mess." Isobel stood in the middle of the room with her hands on her hips. If she'd had an *Englisch* wedding, she would not have been expected to lift a finger on her special day, but Amish weddings were very different. Both Mary and her grandmother had told her that the bride and groom often stay overnight in the very same house they were married in so they could help with the cleaning the next day. It seemed unbelievable but that's the way things were.

"*Jah*, well, we'll do this tomorrow." He pulled Isobel over toward the couch that was still pushed to the side of the room to make way for all the tables of food. "Come, let's sit for a while."

Isobel wondered if Hosea was angry with her. "Are you cross with me for not sending a letter to Emma?"

"*Nee*, I will not be angry with my wife on our wedding night. You did what you thought was best. Emma might be upset, but *Gott* will be with her. Let's not concern ourselves with others tonight, Mrs. Schrock."

Isobel giggled at the sound of her new name. She kept thinking of Mrs. Schrock as Hosea's mother, but now she would have to get used to it being her name as well.

Hosea put his arm around her shoulders. "Did you enjoy our wedding?"

CHAPTER 32

Isobel leaned into him. "It was the nicest wedding I've been to."

"How many have you been to?"

"A few, maybe five, but never an Amish wedding."

Hosea laughed. "I went to five in one day once. We have three to go to next week. The wedding season gets very busy."

"Did you see Mary and Caleb speaking to each other?" Isobel wasn't sure why she wanted to match Mary up with someone. Maybe it was guilt over her being the one to marry Hosea, or maybe she genuinely wanted Mary to be happy.

"They seemed to be getting along."

"Maybe there'll be another wedding soon."

Hosea moved uncomfortably. "I don't know about that. Caleb has got close to two girls and never married either of them. I don't know if he's too interested in having a family any time soon. He's a thinker, and will take a long time to choose someone."

In the short time that Isobel had been in the community, she'd never heard of an Amish person not wanting a family and considered it quite odd. "Have you spoken to him about it?"

"*Nee*, it's none of my business." Hosea held her tighter and said softly, "Thank you for marrying me, Isobel."

Isobel looked into his blue eyes. "Thank you for asking."

They sat quietly for a while and then Hosea said, "Your

CHAPTER 32

grandmother will most likely be asleep already. Let's go to bed."

Hosea's warm, moist breath on Isobel's neck caused her to giggle. "Okay."

Hosea led Isobel upstairs to the room Isobel had carefully prepared for their first night together as a married couple. Isobel fell asleep in Hosea's strong arms, feeling loved, protected and, for the first time in her life, safe.

～

When Isobel woke the next morning, she stretched her arm out to Hosea, but he was gone. She sat upright and touched the spot where he'd slept, and it was cold. Isobel wasn't happy to wake up alone on the first morning as a married couple. Surely it was a bad omen. She had expected to wake up the same way she had fallen asleep—in his arms.

Loud noises coming from the kitchen made Isobel feel guilty for not waking up at the crack of dawn to help with the clean-up.

Oh well, it was too late now to make a good impression. She pulled the bed covers up over her head, determined to have a few more moments in bed. As she closed her heavy eyelids, Emma's horrid interruption of the wedding replayed in her mind. She'd totally ruined the wedding.

Yesterday she'd been concerned about Emma's feelings, but today Isobel was angry with her. Her wedding day had been planned to the last detail, and there was no room for an angry woman to charge in and tell everyone to stop the proceedings.

What right did she have to do that? Hosea had never even taken Emma on a buggy ride and had never even told her that he liked her. It was clear that Emma had a silly crush on Hosea, and that was all. A silly girlish crush. Whatever relationship Emma thought she had with Hosea was entirely in her own head.

Isobel squirmed in bed and held her head.

She would have to apologize to *Mammi* and tell her side of the story. Isobel hoped that her grandmother would forgive her; she did not want things to be awkward now that she and Hosea would be living there for a while.

As she lay alone in bed, Isobel wondered if she should be concerned that Hosea hadn't stayed there until she woke. Was he angry with her?

Isobel heard the bedroom door creak open. She threw back the covers and saw Hosea carrying in a large tray of breakfast. "Hosea, wow, *denke.*" Isobel sat up while Hosea placed the tray on the bed beside her. Isobel was relieved that her fears were unfounded. "Are you coming back to bed?"

"*Nee. Mammi* is doing a lot of cleaning up down there, and I don't want to leave her alone with it all. Not when we told her we'd do it last night. She couldn't have been too happy waking up to see it still there." He leaned over and kissed her forehead. "You stay and eat. Come down when you're ready."

CHAPTER 32

Isobel looked into his eyes and was certain she was the luckiest woman in the world. She corrected her thoughts; she was the most blessed woman in the world. She did not see any disappointment or anything of the sort in his eyes this morning. He kissed her forehead and then walked out the door.

She was now satisfied that he wasn't upset with her. She looked down at the two poached eggs, bacon, fried sweet potatoes, and buttered toast. It was her favorite breakfast, and he knew it.

She picked up the coffee and took a sip. It had a dash of milk just like always. Everything was perfect.

They wouldn't go on a honeymoon like the *Englishers* do. Neither would they visit relatives for weeks after their wedding as many of the newly wed Amish couples did. Hosea had to go back to work immediately, and Isobel would stay home and learn more about their culture.

CHAPTER 33

WEEKS LATER.

Emma opened her eyes and surveyed the room. She had not been dreaming; she was still in her mother and Frank's place, and Isobel was living an improved version of her life. The longing for her grandmother's house and the comfort of her own bedroom welled up inside of her.

Every morning for the first eighteen years of her life, she had woken up in her cozy bedroom to see the rocking chair facing the bed and the cedar dresser that her grandfather made years before. He also made the two matching cedar nightstands by her bed. Emma had never met him, but from the things her grandmother told her, Emma felt as though she knew him very well. Her grandfather had been a talented furniture maker and had made practically every piece of furniture in *Mammi's* house.

The bedroom she had at her mother's was a stark contrast to the comfort of her bedroom back at the farmhouse. There was no furniture in the cold room except for

CHAPTER 33

the oversized bed. An enormous walk-in wardrobe housed all sizes of shelves and drawers. There was enough hanging space to fit the clothes of two families. The bed was comfortable, though, and she was glad of that.

When the time came for Emma to have her own home, she would buy handcrafted Amish furniture with dovetailed drawers, not modern furniture, which was glued together and most likely would not last one generation. She would pass her furniture to her kin if she were blessed with any.

Emma did want to get married, but she had never considered getting married to anyone other than Hosea.

Thinking about her future, her thoughts turned to Travis. She had feelings for him, but it was hard to switch off Hosea and shift her feelings to Travis.

From the noises downstairs, Emma guessed that Frank was leaving for work. She knew that he always left early, and her mother stayed in bed and did not get up until around ten.

Once the noises in the house stopped, and she heard one of the cars leave the garage, she got out of bed, pulled on her robe, and ventured downstairs. She intended to have a few quiet moments in the house to herself before her mother woke.

The kitchen, like everything else in the house, was large and modern. Everything in the kitchen was white or stainless steel. The stove was steel with way too many hot plates and an oversized range hood hovered over the stove.

CHAPTER 33

A large marble island was set in the middle of the floor with three large, clear glass lights hanging low over it. The lights reminded Emma of large lilies with the trumpet part facing downward. Four white stools stood against the island. Emma pulled one of the stools out and sat down, facing the white cappuccino maker. If only she knew how to use it. She could use a coffee right now.

"Good morning."

Emma heard the voice behind her. Emma turned to see her mom in a sleeveless tee and cropped leggings. "Mom, you're awake."

"Yes, I'm going to the gym in the mornings from now on. Would you like to come with me?"

Emma gave a little laugh. "No, thank you."

"It's not that bad." Her mother looked her up and down. "You don't have to worry about your figure, but at my age, things start to sag. Maybe I should've started earlier."

"You don't look like you're sagging."

Her mother scoffed. "Don't get me started on that subject. Coffee?"

"Yes, please." To Emma, her mother looked slim and beautiful, but her mother always found one fault after another with herself.

"I'll make you some toast before I go." As her mother fiddled around in the kitchen, she said, "You know you can stay here as long as you like, don't you?"

"Thanks, Mom. I just don't know what to do with myself yet, but I'll figure it out soon."

CHAPTER 33

"Maybe you should make an appointment with one of those career advisors?"

Emma shrugged her shoulders. "Maybe."

"Frank could always give you a job in his firm if you'd like. I'm sure he'd be able to find something for you. Filing, or sending messages, or something."

"No thanks, I don't want to ask him for any favors." Emma still did not know exactly what Frank did. She knew that he sold insurance but knew nothing other than that.

"He likes you."

Emma searched her mother's face. "He does?"

"Yes, I'm sure he does, in his own way."

"I don't mean to be rude, Mom, but he's only putting up with me for your sake. That's plain to see. It's nice of him, though, and I appreciate it."

After her mother frothed the milk for the coffees and poured it into the two waiting mugs, she said, "You've got him all wrong. Frank just doesn't waste energy on emotion. He does have emotions."

A knock on the door interrupted their conversation.

"That'll be the housekeeper. She's only here a half day today." Her mother left the room to let the housekeeper in.

Emma smiled. Her mom's life was so different now from the Amish life in which she'd been raised. The traditional Amish would not consider having someone else clean their home, not when they weren't working outside the home. There was nothing very traditional about her

CHAPTER 33

mother, though, and Emma could not even imagine her mother being raised by her strict grandmother; the two of them were complete opposites.

Mom returned to the room and picked up her coffee. "What's the smile for?"

"Just thinking about how back home, no one has a housekeeper."

Mom gave a little grunt. "I couldn't wait to leave the Amish."

"Why? What was so bad about it?" Emma had never spoken in depth about the past. They were getting used to each other in the present, and Emma was too nervous to speak of the past in case it brought back bad memories for her mother.

"I can't even think where to start. It was too restrictive. I wanted to do what I liked without a thousand sets of eyes on me." Her mother shuddered and grunted her disapproval, and then she sat on the stool next to Emma.

"I don't think it's like that, Mom. People are just concerned and watching out for each other."

"Are you thinking of going back there, back to the Amish?"

Emma laughed. "I can't now. I'm just so embarrassed after the big scene I created at the wedding. Also, it would be too hard to see Hosea with someone else."

Her mother looked down into her coffee. "Yes, it must be hard for you."

Emma glanced sideways at her mother. Even just for going to the gym, her face was flawlessly made up. Her

CHAPTER 33

thick wavy hair was secured at the back of her head in a topknot.

Her mother took a sip of coffee and then stood up. "I'll be at the gym for about an hour, and then I'm going on to lunch with some girlfriends. So, I'll see you very late this afternoon."

"I'm seeing Travis tonight. We arranged that already."

"Okay, well, I might not see you at all then." Her mother tipped the remainder of her coffee down the sink and then kissed Emma on her forehead before she left.

To avoid the housekeeper, who was vacuuming the carpets in the living room, Emma took her coffee back to her room. She sat on her bed and thought about Travis. She was looking forward to seeing him and was surprised that she had tiny butterflies in her stomach at the thought of him.

With her cup of coffee in her hand, Emma looked out the bedroom window into the garden. Her mother's two fluffy white dogs were fighting over a chew toy. Emma couldn't help smiling at their antics. What useless little creatures they are, she thought. Emma was used to bigger dogs at the farm, dogs that were of some useful purpose. Then Emma noticed the chairs and table in the corner of the garden where the morning sun shone.

Just the spot for me to sit and relax for a bit.

As soon as Emma walked outside, the dogs jumped up on her, scratching her legs. She opened the back door, called them over, and pushed them inside.

"Miss, do you mind if I keep the dogs upstairs while I

CHAPTER 33

clean downstairs?" Emma heard the voice of the cleaner and turned to see her just inside the door.

"Yes, of course." Emma's mother often kept the dogs upstairs restricted by a dog gate at the top. With just the press of a button, a gate would appear at the top of the stairs and attach to the side wall.

Alone in the garden, Emma tucked her legs underneath and made herself comfortable in the plush, cushioned seat. She closed her eyes and turned her face toward the sun, letting the heat sink deeply into her skin. After a few moments, she realized that this was the first time in a long time that she had truly relaxed. She did not have to pretend to be someone she wasn't.

∼

Emma met Travis outside Isobel's old apartment building. She hadn't told him she was staying at her mother's place. It was easier just to meet him there.

Thankfully, he was always on time; that was one of the many things Emma liked about him. Emma saw him walking toward her on the tic of seven o'clock just as they had arranged. She gave him a small wave, and as he smiled at her, her tummy fluttered a little.

As he stood before her, there was an awkward moment between the both of them. He leaned in to kiss her cheek, and she moved away. "I'm sorry. I'm just—"

"No need to apologize. Where would you like to go tonight?" Travis asked.

CHAPTER 33

"You don't have to keep meeting me like this. I'm not Isobel."

"Hey, you're you. I like being with you. So where do you want to go?"

"Anywhere you want. I like most food."

"I know a good Chinese restaurant."

"That sounds perfect."

Travis hailed a taxi.

"Not taking your car?"

"Never. Parking is a nightmare in the city. It's easier this way."

As they sat together in the back seat of the taxi, Emma could scarcely breathe. She liked Travis but didn't know what to do. She shouldn't have swerved away from his kiss just now. It was just a hello kiss and they'd been seeing each other regularly for weeks.

Emma was sure that Travis noticed she was acting odd, but he didn't say anything.

She waited until after they had begun to eat to speak. "I've got something to tell you, Travis."

Travis put his chopsticks down and clasped his fingers together. "I thought you'd been quieter than usual. What is it?"

Emma put her head down, and a wave of heat swept over her body. "Let's go outside. I think I need some air."

Travis told the waiter they were going outside for a moment and they'd be back. Travis took Emma's hand and led her outside.

CHAPTER 33

As they stood in the cool night air, Travis said, "Are you going to make me guess?"

Emma shook her head. She found it hard to look into his soft, brown eyes, but she made herself. "The truth of it all is that I don't know what's going on with you and me. Are we friends, or… are we on a date? What is this?"

"What do you want it to be?"

Emma smiled. "That's not a fair answer. You seem to have taken the news that Isobel got married quite well."

He looked down at the ground, then he looked back at her with a grin and raised eyebrows.

Her skin flushed. "What's funny?"

"I do have a confession to make if you won't be mad at me."

"What is it?" Emma asked.

"You won't be upset?"

She frowned. "Depends on what you're about to tell me."

He raised a finger in the air. "Ah, now that's not fair."

"Stop it, Travis. Just tell me."

"I'd already guessed you weren't Isobel way before you told me. At Isobel's wedding, I was just playing along. I should've told you before now."

"What? How did you find out? And when did you know?" She raised her hands in the air, and he grabbed hold of them. Then he gave a low chuckle.

"Isobel told me a long time ago that she had an identical twin. You had me fooled that first day, and then I caught on." His eyes sparkled with mischief.

CHAPTER 33

She recalled he wasn't that shocked at Isobel's wedding. He certainly wasn't devastated like she was. "How did you figure out that I wasn't Isobel?"

He stared into her face. "The accent that you try too hard to cover up, the lapses of memory, the different expression on your face when you look at me, and those five freckles on your face that Isobel never had." He smiled. "You made a good effort at it, though, I must say. You're a good actress."

Emma thought back to all those moments. "Why didn't you ever say anything?"

"I didn't want to ruin anything. I enjoyed our time together with you pretending to be Isobel. Especially when you agreed with me on things that Isobel would never have agreed with."

Emma felt the heat rise in her cheeks as she pried her eyes away from his intense gaze. "You're making fun of me."

"I'm not, believe me. I'm not. I didn't say anything to you because I didn't want to scare you away."

"Travis, there's so much you don't know about me. I'm not like other girls. I've never had a boyfriend before."

"That's okay, isn't it?"

"I'm still Amish on the inside. Just because I'm not living in the community doesn't mean that my heart's not there. I do want to live by *Gott's* ways."

"Do you need to be living back in the community to do that?"

"I think I do. It would be easier." Emma breathed out

heavily. "Travis, I need to ask you something important. I need the truth, and I won't be upset."

"Go on. I've got nothing to hide."

"What caused you and Isobel to stop dating? Why was she upset when she came to see me?"

"I thought I explained all that with you when you were pretending to be Isobel."

"Tell me again."

"She saw me with a girl and jumped to conclusions."

"Is that all?"

"Yes. Ask her if you want. She'll tell you the same thing. Although, she won't admit to letting her mind run away with her."

"You knew I was me then? I mean, you knew I wasn't Isobel way back then?"

He nodded.

Emma took hold of Travis' hand. "And you still want to be friends?"

"Yes."

"I'm hungry. Let's eat."

Once they sat back at the table, Travis stared at her. "You won't disappear on me, will you?"

Emma had just bitten into an egg roll, and her mouth was full, so she shook her head and smiled.

"I've grown fond of you. No, more than fond. I'll break down those walls you've got up." Travis gave her a wink, which caused her insides to quiver.

CHAPTER 33

The next day, Emma thought it only fair that Jade, Isobel's best friend, should know that she and Isobel had traded places.

If Isobel had turned her back on her twin, she would think nothing of turning her back on her friends.

Emma arranged to meet with Jade in a coffee shop. She'd not spoken to her in person since she'd returned from Isobel's wedding.

Jade sat quietly and listened to all that Emma had to say. "You mean to tell me that you aren't Isobel, you're her twin?"

Emma nodded.

"That makes a lot of sense." Jade's black-tipped fingernails drummed on her bottom lip. "That's why you had that book with everything written in it? There was nothing wrong with your memory at all, was there?"

Emma recalled the awful day at the hospital after her panic attack. Jade was looking for her phone to call Emma's mother, and she found Isobel's notebook in Emma's bag. She'd had to do a lot of fast-talking to convince Jade that she was having memory lapses. "Yes, Isobel wrote it for me so I would know everything about her life."

"And now Isobel's married?" Jade's face turned white, amplifying her heavily made-up, black-rimmed eyes and black lips.

"Yes, exactly."

Jade shook her head. "No, she would've told me. We're best friends."

CHAPTER 33

"It's true. I was at the wedding myself." Emma wondered whether Isobel intended to continue her friendship with Jade. Isobel might want to keep her distance from her *English* friend who had a pierced nose, wore black lipstick, and always wore black clothes.

Jade raised her eyebrows so high that light lines appeared on her forehead. "I just don't believe it. She'd never marry an Amish man. For a start, she loved the city."

"She never told you about her and my swapping places, did she? She doesn't tell you everything." Emma did not want to upset Jade; she just wanted her to know the truth. It would have been much easier if Isobel had called Jade and told her. Surely Isobel could have done that by now.

"But she was in love with Travis. They were always having disagreements, so I never took them seriously."

"She came to me because she was upset with Travis. She said she was heartbroken. That's why she wanted me to swap places with her. Then she met Hosea."

"And she's really in love with this guy, Hosea?"

"Yes."

"Why wouldn't she tell me what she was planning? I would've supported her in anything she wanted to do."

"I don't know. Maybe she decided to go to see me on the spur of the moment."

"Yeah, possibly." Jade nodded and had a faraway look in her eyes. "Poor Travis. How's he doing? Have you seen him?"

"I have. He was shocked at first, but he's getting over

CHAPTER 33

it." She didn't tell Jade that she had feelings for Travis. "Do you think Isobel was a good match with Travis?"

"Yes. I thought they'd be together forever, but it seems I was wrong."

"Do you think Travis is trustworthy?"

Jade looked up at her. "One hundred percent. There should be more guys around like him."

Emma was pleased to hear it.

Jade studied Emma's face. "Oh, Emma, you like him."

Emma couldn't keep the smile from her face. "A little bit."

"That's insane."

"Why?" Emma asked.

Jade laughed. "Nothing."

"Can you tell me about Travis?" Emma asked.

The waiter who came to take their order interrupted them.

Jade picked up the menu and had a quick look. "I'll just have a black coffee and a piece of carrot cake, please."

"Ahh, same for me, thanks."

When the waitress left, Jade leaned forward. "I can tell you he's reliable. He's good husband material that's why I'm surprised Isobel let him go. Is this just a joke? Are you really Emma or are you Isobel? Wait, it's not April so it can't be April Fool's day."

Emma laughed. "I am Emma."

"I can't believe I never noticed the difference. A good friend would've noticed. I was too wrapped up in my own life. Isobel probably knew that, and that's why she never confided in me. I'm going to visit her as soon as I can."

"She'd love that."

"Do you think so?"

"Of course," Emma said.

CHAPTER 34

Isobel squinted at the light streaming in through the window of her bedroom. She stepped closer and looked at her reflection in the windowpane. Having no mirrors in the *house*, the window was the only way she could really see how she looked. *I'll never get used to this stupid 'no mirror thing.' When I have my own home, I'll insist on having at least one mirror*; surely, *there's no harm in that.*

It was difficult for Isobel not to be concerned about her looks. She was wearing plain unflattering large dresses the same as all the women in the community. Although she wasn't supposed to wear makeup, she always applied base foundation, which no one seemed to mind, and if they did, they kept it to themselves.

After a time with no Internet and no cell phone, Isobel had found that she did not miss either since chores and other activities had taken their place. People in the

CHAPTER 34

community often visited, and their social life filled in any free time.

Isobel had chosen to immerse herself in Amish culture, and what better place to start than a quilting bee? Though she'd never quilted or sewn before, the intricate patterns of traditional Amish quilts called out to her. Her grandmother gifted her and Hosea with a lavish quilt for their wedding gift, but Isobel saw no problem with having two, so she decided to make another one.

∽

There were mostly older women at the quilting bee, along with a couple of younger women, including Mary. Mary and Isobel had become a little closer after the wedding, and Isobel was still determined to match-make her with Caleb, Hosea's brother.

Isobel had no material and had not even chosen a pattern. Today, she was there to observe. Next week she would choose an easy quilt pattern, and someone would show her what to do.

Once the quilting bee was underway, Isobel was left out of the conversation, which was mainly about people she did not know, until Mary asked her about Caleb. Isobel was delighted that Mary was showing an interest. And why wouldn't she? He was one of the most handsome single Amish bachelors in their community.

Mary took her half-made quilt out of her bag and spread it over her knees. "Don't start out making a whole quilt first. Start with something simple, like a potholder," she advised Isobel.

Isobel screwed up her nose. "Do you think?" Isobel liked to get stuck into things straight away. Surely it was a waste of time to make a small article first.

Mary nodded, and the women murmured their agreement at Mary's suggestion.

"I suppose I will then."

"So, Isobel, do you know Caleb very well?" Mary asked. "I mean as well as you can for only being here a short while? You must've spent time with him, *jah?*"

"He's very quiet. He's had a couple of girlfriends but nothing very serious, I'm told."

"Oh, he's a *gut* catch, Mary," one of the older ladies said.

Mary giggled. "I do like him, but please, no one say anything to him. That would only embarrass me."

"I'll invite him to dinner next week, and you can come too," Isobel said, hoping that *Mammi* would not mind her inviting people to dinner without asking.

"That would be *wunderbaar,* Isobel, *denke.*"

"Don't you think that he's too old for you, dear?" Another of the older ladies said.

"Not at all. I like mature men."

All the ladies giggled. Isobel saw for herself that the quilting bees were part sewing and part gossip, which she didn't mind in the least.

CHAPTER 34

Mammi was delighted when Isobel told her that she had invited Caleb and Mary for the evening meal.

"They sat together at my wedding and seemed to get along just fine. The only thing is, Hosea thinks that Caleb isn't too keen on the idea of getting married," Isobel told her grandmother.

Mammi tossed her head back and scoffed. "All men make out they aren't interested when they haven't found the right one. He wouldn't want to appear that he's not been successful with women, would he?"

Isobel thought what she said made sense. "I suppose you're right."

"*Jah*, I am right. He'd be interested in women and hopefully interested in Mary."

Isobel was surprised at how she and her grandmother had bonded over the past months. *Mammi* didn't even seem to care too much about her and Emma switching places. "I'll do the cooking, *Mammi*, and give you a break."

"*Nee*, I like to cook."

Isobel laughed. "Well, I'll help you then."

"Okay, we'll have Swiss steak, roast chicken, roast vegetables, and coleslaw."

"That sounds perfect. I'll make a blueberry pie for dessert."

~

Just before Mary and Caleb arrived for dinner, Hosea came up behind Isobel as she was cooking the steak. He placed his hands on her shoulders and whispered, "Don't work too hard to try to put the two of them together. These things should happen by themselves."

Isobel swung around and saw the concern on his face. "I just invited the two of them to dinner, and then the rest is up to them. I've got nothing else up my sleeve. See?" She pulled on the end of her long sleeve and lifted it up.

Hosea raised his eyebrows and chuckled.

Isobel laughed too. "Aren't you pleased I'm trying to help your *bruder*?"

"I'm not saying that."

"Well, don't you want your brother to be happy like you are?" As usual, Isobel blurted out her words without thinking. Maybe Hosea wasn't happy being married, and he did not want Caleb to be hasty in marriage as he had been.

"It's not what I want for him; it's what he wants for himself that's important. Nothing good ever comes from meddling."

Hosea's words were like a knife to her heart. She wanted him to think that everything she did was excellent, but he thought of her matchmaking as nothing more than meddling. That was hurtful when she was only doing it from the kindness of her heart.

Isobel turned her back to Hosea and remained silent, so he would not see the tear that slowly trickled down her cheek.

He stepped closer. "Why are you crying?"

CHAPTER 34

"You've upset me." Now she was more upset because he had to ask why she was crying. He should've known.

"I didn't mean to. I'm sorry if I said something to upset you, but I don't want anyone to be uncomfortable tonight. I don't want them to think we're pushing them together."

Isobel could not tolerate any more criticism. At that moment, she did not care if Hosea saw the tears running down her face or if he saw the anger in her flushed cheeks. "All right, I get your point." Isobel left the food and walked right out of the kitchen.

Several minutes later, Isobel looked out her bedroom window and saw Hosea walking over to the barn. She hurried back downstairs to help with the meal.

As she prepared the pastry for the blueberry pie, she wondered whether she should be trying to match Emma with Caleb rather than Mary.

"You're very quiet, Isobel."

Isobel looked up to see that her grandmother had walked into the kitchen, and she hadn't even noticed; she was too busy with the pastry and watching the food on the stove. "Oh, I was hoping Mary and Caleb would get along with each other at dinner tonight."

"You get the liking of matchmaking from me. Remember when Hosea's grandmother and I tried to match you and Hosea?" *Mammi* chuckled.

"*Jah*, but you thought that I was Emma at the time." Isobel sent up a silent prayer of thanks that she and

Mammi got along so well even though their relationship had begun with deception.

Mammi gave another laugh. "Well, it worked. The two of you are very happy."

Isobel licked her lips. "Would you have preferred Emma to marry Hosea?"

"*Nee*, Hosea made his choice. The two of you loved him, and he chose you. Only one of you could be his wife." *Mammi* put her arm around Isobel's waist and hugged her. "Never you mind about looking to the past. It's the present you need to live in; the past can't be changed, but you can change your future by minding what you do in the present."

Isobel was comforted by her grandmother's wise words. She knew that *Gott* did not hold someone's past against them when they asked for forgiveness. Isobel had asked forgiveness for anything wrong she'd done toward Emma. Of course, now she would have to ask for Emma's forgiveness at some point. But that was a concern for another day.

That evening, Caleb arrived at the house first. Isobel couldn't help but notice how handsome he was. He'd put some effort into his neat and tidy appearance. Caleb had the same dark eyes and dark hair as Hosea, but his age was apparent in his face, which had etched lines at the corners of his eyes and faint lines across his forehead. "Hello, Caleb. We have Mary coming for dinner as well, Mary Miller."

"*Jah*, I know, Hosea told me."

CHAPTER 34

Isobel considered that he looked a little nervous. He normally seemed sure of himself. Isobel showed him into the house, and he greeted Hosea who was in the living room.

As soon as Caleb sat on the couch with Hosea, Isobel heard another horse and buggy clip-clopping its way up to the house. Isobel walked out to meet Mary.

Mary stopped at the house and then tied her horse to the hitching post. "Hi Isobel. He's here already, is he?" Mary's eyes were fixed on Caleb's horse and buggy.

"*Jah*, he's only just arrived."

Isobel quickly ushered Mary inside. As soon as Mary and Caleb exchanged greetings, Isobel knew that she had done the right thing. She shot a look to Hosea that said, *I told you so*, and he looked away with no acknowledgment.

Over the meal, the conversation was a little forced, but it did have the desired effect. Mary and Caleb were talking to each other and seemed to be getting along.

When the evening was over, and Caleb was halfway up the road in his buggy, Mary ran back into the *house* and whispered in Isobel's ear, "He asked me out on a date, a real date."

"That's great, Mary."

"*Jah*, he asked me to help him choose a new buggy, but I guess that's a date. What do you think?"

"Are you sure?"

"Are you a buggy expert?"

Mary giggled. "No."

Mary glanced over at Hosea, who was studying the

both of them from the living room. "I'll go now. I just wanted to tell you that."

"That's great, Mary. Let me know how it goes." Isobel stood at the door and waited until Mary turned her buggy around and headed down the road.

When Isobel closed the door, Hosea said, "Did you have success with your scheme?"

"*Jah*. Caleb has asked Mary out. The night went exactly how I wanted."

Hosea raised his eyebrows a little and said nothing. Isobel had never seen Mary look so happy in all the time she'd known her. She did not care if Hosea approved of her matchmaking or not. It was worth a little disapproval from him to see the happiness on her friend's face.

CHAPTER 35

Emma reached the point where she had to know the truth about her father. She arranged to have lunch at home with her mother and had asked for her full attention insisting she turn off her cell phone.

Emma had prepared her mother's favorite chicken Caesar salad. Once they were seated, Emma jumped in rather than meandering around the point. "Mom, you've never told me who my father is."

Her mother's hand flew to her throat. "No, and that's something that's not relevant right now. It doesn't matter who he is."

"Does Isobel know anything about him? She told me she doesn't know anything, but maybe she wasn't being truthful."

Mom shook her head. "No, she has no need to know him."

"I think we both have a right to know who he is at the

CHAPTER 35

very least." Emma considered it crucial to know who her father was if she were to figure out who she was. She had to have that information before she could make plans for her future.

"Just leave it alone, Emma." Mom stood up and walked out of the room, leaving her barely touched salad behind.

Emma didn't go after her. She wasn't going to get any information from her today.

There was only one thing for it.

She'd have to wait until everyone had left the house and then she'd search for her birth certificate. Hopefully, it was in the house, and the father would be named. Frank's den was the best place to start. That's where her mother kept some of her jewelry, so it was a likely place to keep important paperwork.

Emma did not have to wait long.

Mom drove away from the house without letting Emma know where she was going. They hadn't spoken a word since Emma had asked about her birth father. Frank wasn't due home for another three hours.

After having no luck in Frank's den, Emma moved to her mother's bedroom.

Emma climbed up to the top shelf of her mother's walk-in wardrobe and found a small wooden box. It was the perfect size to keep paperwork. She took the box down and placed it on a chair. She quickly pulled off the lid and saw a lot of old papers.

Her heart beat a little faster. As she rifled through, she

CHAPTER 35

saw her mother's old work references, employment records, and a couple of old bank statements.

Then she came across an unmarked envelope. Emma held the envelope in her hands. Could this contain the birth certificates? She took a deep breath, pulled the papers out of the envelope, and carefully unfolded them.

They were her and Isobel's birth certificates!

Emma blew out a deep breath before she looked any further.

She held the two documents side by side. The first thing Emma saw was the times of their births. It didn't surprise her to learn Isobel was born ten minutes earlier than she. Somehow Emma already knew Isobel was the older twin.

She looked at the name of their father and was pleased to see that there was a name, and it did not just say 'father unknown.' The name on the certificate, listed as their father, was Kelvin Young.

"Kelvin Young," Emma said the name out loud. She did not recognize the name. From the information on the birth certificate, he was forty-two years of age at the time of their birth, and his profession was listed as 'Investment Banker.'

Emma folded the certificates back into the envelope. "Forty-two, that's a bit old when mom was only eighteen. What was she thinking?" Emma decided to look through the other papers to see if Kelvin's name was mentioned on anything else. It was then that she found the same name,

CHAPTER 35

Kelvin Young, on an old employment reference. The reference was dated back to a year after she was born.

The paper fell from her hands. Did her mother have twins with her employer, the one who was married with other children?

That would explain a lot, especially the secrecy.

Emma closed her eyes and tried to remember exactly what her mother had said about her employer from when she and Isobel were born. He'd told her mother that she could only keep one baby if she wanted to keep her job.

But if they were his twins…

"What are you doing in here?"

Emma jumped up off the bed and looked up to see her mother's scowling face. Then her mother's gaze fixed on the open wooden box, which was on the chair.

Mom lunged at the box and then noticed the other paperwork. She grabbed everything and placed it back in the box, and closed it. "What did you see, Emma?"

Emma stared at the ground, ashamed to go against her mother's wishes. At the same time, she now knew the truth. "I know who my father is. I had to find out."

Rose put the box back in the cupboard. She turned around and glared at Emma. "I'm ashamed of you snooping amongst my things. Shame on you."

"No, Mom. Shame on you for having an affair with a married man." Emma glared back at her mother.

"What do you mean?"

"I saw that he was the man you worked for, and you told me he said you could only keep one baby." Anger overtook Emma, anger at her mother for being so stupid to get involved with a married man, and anger at her father for letting her mother give her away as if she were nothing. "How could you be so stupid to have an affair with a married man, Mom? I mean, where did you see that going?"

Her mother fell to her knees on the floor and wept.

Emma had never seen her mother weak and vulnerable. She kneeled beside her and put her arm around her. "I didn't mean to be so horrid to you. Everyone makes mistakes."

Her mother tried to talk, but no words came out.

She patted her mother on the back as she blinked back tears of her own.

After her mother had stopped crying, she managed to say, "It wasn't an affair. He forced me."

Emma's whole body froze. She stood up and then sank to the bed in disbelief.

Her mother continued, "He said if I told anyone, he'd deny it, and make sure I'd get no work anywhere else. I was too ashamed to go back home to my mother after what had happened. Months later, I found out I was pregnant."

"I'd rather not know." The words spilled out of Emma's mouth before she could stop them, but it was true. She wished she hadn't been curious. The truth was far worse than not knowing at all.

Her mother wiped her eyes with the back of her hand. "Now you know why I don't speak about the past."

CHAPTER 35

"Sorry I didn't leave things alone, but I'm still pleased to know the truth. I think I am anyway." That explained how her mother was able to block her out for eighteen years. Her father sounded harsh and awful, and Emma realized that Isobel must have taken after him. How else could she have stolen Hosea from her in such a cruel way?

"Do you still want to meet him?" her mother asked.

"No, I don't want to meet a man like that, even if he is my father." Emma took a couple of deep breaths. "Does his wife know what he did?"

"No, I'm sure that she never suspected a thing. Not a thing. He was too good at being manipulative, and he's a good liar."

"I'm sorry that you had to go through such a terrible thing all alone."

Her mother patted her hand. "I stayed there until Isobel was about one, and then I got a job with another family. It was there that I studied at night and was able to get a better job." She sniffed a couple of times. "I didn't come back to get you because you had settled in with *Mammi* and that was the only home you'd ever known. To be truthful, I had a selfish reason. If I had visited, it would've been too hard for me to leave again. I couldn't visit and leave you a second time."

Emma hugged her mother tightly. "In my heart, there was a reason for what you did. I understand, Mom. I know." For the first time, Emma saw with her own eyes how hard it had been for her mother. "The bishop always says not to judge someone. I can see the reason behind that now. You can't judge someone because there are always things you don't know from the other person's point of view."

"Yes, I suppose that's true enough."

"I was so upset with you, but now it makes some sense to me."

Her mother wiped her eyes. "It was hard for everyone."

"What did Frank say about what that man did to you?"

Her mother looked into Emma's eyes and said, "Frank knows nothing. He guessed that something happened to me, but I've never told him, and he hasn't pushed me to tell him."

"Maybe you should tell him."

"I'm afraid of what he'd do. He might be silly enough to try and take some kind of revenge."

"Surely not, would he?" Emma knew that Frank was rich, but he was no gangster.

Her mother shrugged her shoulders. "I don't know. He has some powerful friends."

"You'd feel better if you told him."

"I'll think about it."

"I don't like to see you upset like this." Emma always thought of her mother as somewhat cold, but now she could see that she'd done her best in bad circumstances. She helped her mother to her feet, and then they both sat on the bed.

"I'll be all right, Emma. I might tell Frank now that you know. I guess he deserves to know everything. He's been so good to me all these years."

CHAPTER 35

Emma smiled and nodded, but all she could think about was telling Travis.

Hours later, Emma called Travis to arrange to meet later that evening. It was then that she realized that the closest person to her—her best friend in the world was Travis.

～

Travis picked up Emma at the house, and they went for a drive. Emma felt better just being in his company.

They hadn't gotten far up the road when Travis glanced over at her. "What's up, Emma? I feel you've got something you want to say."

"I don't know if Isobel ever told you, but we never knew who our father was."

"No, she didn't discuss that with me. I never thought to ask."

"Well, Mom wouldn't tell me, so I snooped around her room and found our birth certificates."

"Go on." Travis glanced at Emma every now and again while trying to keep his eyes on the road.

"It's so horrible. It's too horrible to even say."

"Wait. I'll stop the car." Travis swerved the car over to the side of the road and turned to face her. "Nothing can be that horrible. Just tell me."

She took a deep breath and continued, "When my mother was young, she was a live-in housemaid and babysitter." Emma paused for a moment. "When she

CHAPTER 35

found she was having twins, the employer said that she could only have one baby at the house. So, if she wanted to keep her job, she couldn't do it with both of us."

"That's horrible. I guess she had to make that choice if she had no other means of financial support."

"There's more."

Travis saw how upset she was and leaned over and took hold of her hand.

"It was the employer's name on the birth certificate. He's our father."

Travis made a face. "Really?"

"Mom said that he forced himself on her."

Travis' jaw dropped. "Emma, he should be charged and locked up."

"It was so long ago, though. I don't know if the police would be interested."

"Doesn't matter. He can still be charged. Has Rose thought about pressing charges?"

Emma shook her head. "No, she wouldn't. She feels too shameful about the whole thing."

"Does Isobel know?"

"No, you are the only person who knows. You and that horrible man – and that horrible man is my father."

"No wonder you're so upset." They were silent for a while, then Travis asked, "Are you going to tell Isobel?"

"I don't know. It was awkward how things were left, and she hasn't reached out to me."

"I'll drive you there. Once the two of you know, you can work out if you want to do anything about it. And

CHAPTER 35

someone has to be the first to reach out. Isobel is most likely waiting for you to make the first move."

"Thanks, Travis. You're really the only person in the world that I can rely on. It's probably a good idea to tell her. It's best to know the truth." She looked at him from under her lashes. "But if we go there together, how do you think you'll cope when you see her again?"

Travis smiled and looked deep into her eyes. "I was over Isobel a long time ago. I never think about Isobel anymore. She's in the past."

"Really?"

"I love you, Emma." Travis laughed. "There, I've said it. I've put myself out on a ledge and revealed my feelings."

It warmed Emma's heart to hear his words, but she was not sure that she loved him back. What was love? She knew she wanted to spend all her time with him, and she felt better when he was around, but was that love?

Emma stared into his eyes as he moved his mouth closer to hers. She did not move away when he placed his warm lips over hers.

Travis quickly drew back. "Sorry about that, Emma. I don't know what came over me."

Emma touched her lips. She didn't want him to stop kissing her. "Don't be sorry," was all that she said as he started the car's engine.

CHAPTER 36

Before Isobel had swapped places with Emma, she'd been trapped in a life of materialism. Possessions and clothing labels were all she thought of. Now, she had developed consideration and caring for others. She loved her new life of simplicity, where the focus was on family and loved ones rather than on physical objects.

She decided a baby should come next for herself and Hosea. If she had a baby, she would have someone to love her always. Sometimes she wasn't sure if Hosea still loved her; he said he did, but it wasn't as if he could change his mind about her and get a divorce. Once an Amish person married, there was no going back. She often wondered whether he regretted the hasty marriage and was simply making the best of the situation.

A baby was the solution to bring her husband closer–Isobel was certain of that. Maybe they would even have twins. Hosea had predicted they would buy their own

CHAPTER 36

house in six months, so if she were to fall pregnant now, by the time the baby arrived, they would have their own place.

She decided to pray for twins. Two were always better than one.

∞

The next time Travis and Emma saw each other, they were to arrange a time to visit Isobel.

Travis visited Emma at home, and Emma was thankful that Frank was at work and her mother had just left for the gym.

"It looks like my father's lined up a good job for me next year, and it's not far from your old home," Travis said.

"That's wonderful, Travis." Emma knew that Travis' father was an engineer, and Travis was just about to finish his engineering degree. "Is it with your father's company?"

"No, it's a similar company. And it's run by a friend of his. I could always get a job with Dad's company, but I prefer to do my own thing. I won't say no to him helping me get a job, though." Travis laughed.

"So, is it for sure?"

"Yes, if I want it, the job's mine. I'm going there to meet them next week. That'll be a perfect chance for us to see Isobel to discuss those things you wanted with her."

CHAPTER 36

"That would be wonderful. I was hoping we would do that soon. I'll be able to see my grandmother too."

"And Hosea?" Travis chuckled.

Emma looked down and felt her cheeks warm up. She should never have allowed him to know that she'd liked Hosea, but at the time, she didn't know what Travis meant to her. Emma hoped he would not take that job; she would be quite happy if things stayed just as they were.

∽

Hosea had only just left for work in his horse and buggy when Isobel heard a car pull up outside the *house*. When she heard *Mammi* let out a squeal, Isobel ran to the bedroom window to see who it was. She saw Travis' car, and then she heard Emma's voice before she saw her.

It was Emma and she was with Travis.

Isobel wondered what they wanted. The last thing she wanted was a confrontation.

She hurried out of the bedroom and rushed down the stairs. Her stomach clenched hard when she saw Travis and Emma in the house.

"There you are, Isobel. Travis and I called in to see you and *Mammi* to tell you the news."

Isobel stepped closer, thankful that they weren't there to accuse her of anything. "What news?"

"Travis is starting work here next year, well, not far from here."

"That's *wunderbaar*," Mammi said.

CHAPTER 36

"That's nice." Isobel forced a smile. She hadn't counted on Travis ever living close by. She hoped it wouldn't make Hosea jealous. That would further drive him away.

"Are you staying long?" *Mammi* asked them.

Travis answered, "We're heading back before dark."

"I hope you two don't mind if I speak to Emma alone, do you?" *Mammi* asked.

"Of course not," Isobel said.

Mammi took Emma into the kitchen. "What are you doing, Emma? Are you in a relationship with Travis? Not that I've got anything against him personally, but he's an *Englisher*. Are you coming back to the community or what?"

Emma spoke quietly, "I've got something more important to talk to you about. It's about Mom."

"Really? Is she unwell?"

"*Nee*, she's okay. Did she ever tell you about my father?"

Mammi immediately moved away and looked down. "*Nee*, she never mentioned, and I never asked."

Emma told her what had happened.

Mammi gasped, moved to the table, and sat down. "*Nee, nee*. Poor child." Tears welled in her eyes. "Why didn't she tell me? Why did she keep it from me?"

"She said she couldn't come back to the community because it would bring continual shame upon you."

"And she's lived with that all of these years."

Emma bit her lip and wondered if she should have left

things be and not told her grandmother something so terrible. "I'm sorry, *Mammi*. Perhaps I shouldn't have told you."

"*Nee*, child. You did the right thing. The truth is always revealed in the end. What is covered will be uncovered."

"I'm sorry, *Mammi*. Are you sure you're all right?"

"*Jah*, just sad for what happened to Rose when she was so young. Sad that she had to keep that secret from me for all those years. I had a very different idea of what had happened."

Emma leaned down and put her arm around her grandmother's shoulders. "C'mon, we can't leave these two alone for too long."

Mammi nodded and stood up.

"Ahh, there you both are. Now it's my turn to have a little chat with Emma." Isobel turned to Travis. "You don't mind if I steal her away for a moment, do you?"

"You go right ahead, Isobel," Travis said from the next room.

Isobel walked outside with Emma. Things were so awkward between them. She had to clear the air even if it meant things would be uncomfortable.

CHAPTER 37

"What are you playing at, Emma? Are you dating him because I married Hosea? Do you really love him, or are you trying to get back at me?"

Emma winced at the unexpected exchange. "Yes, of course, I love him."

"You know what he did to me. He can't be trusted."

"He told me about that. The woman was just outside of his apartment building. He was coming out, and she was already there."

"I don't think that's what I saw, but if you trust him, that's your business." Isobel folded her arms across her chest. "Convenient story. Anyway, he never denied anything, and he never mentioned that to me."

"Did you give him a chance to tell you?" Emma asked.

"I guess not. Anyway, I was too upset to listen to his lies. Men always lie, except for Amish men."

"Had Travis ever lied to you before?"

CHAPTER 37

"No, not up until then." Isobel bit her lip. She had jumped to all the wrong conclusions and ran away from Travis for no good reason. It was true that she had never questioned him further on what had happened. She had assumed the worst.

"Well..."

"Yes, yes. I understand your point. No need to keep rubbing it in, Emma. It's a good thing, though, because if I hadn't come here to see you, I wouldn't have met Hosea."

"I know. Do you want to speak with Travis?"

"It doesn't matter now, does it? I'm happily married, and the past is the past. Everything happens for a reason. I'm prepared to forget everything." Isobel swallowed the hard lump that had formed in her throat. "I'm happy for the two of you."

"Thank you."

"Emma, I must apologize to you. I have a heavy heart because I knew that you loved Hosea, and then I married him without telling you. So, I'm very sorry." Isobel could see that Emma's face was like flint. Would it need more than an apology to make her sister forgive her? Isobel breathed out heavily. "I know I can't take it back, but will you ever forgive me?"

Emma sucked in her lips as she kept her eyes fixed on Isobel. "It means a great deal that you said that you're sorry. I think I can forgive you in time. I forgive you in my head, but my heart might take a little time to catch up with my head."

Isobel smiled. "*Denke,* that's a good start. I don't blame

you for being upset." The distance Isobel felt from Hosea played on her mind. In her heart, she hoped that by making things right with Emma, the rest of her life would fall into place.

The twins went back into the house, both feeling better after their talk.

After the midday meal, Emma and Travis decided to take a walk. Isobel felt a pang of jealousy, seeing them happily walking hand in hand. They seemed close, closer than she was with Hosea.

Not only that, but it was the way they looked at each other, exchanging glances, the private little jokes that only the two of them understood. Compared to Emma and Travis's relationship, Isobel considered that her relationship with Hosea had turned cold in a few short months of marriage.

Travis and Emma arrived back at the house from their walk at the same time as Hosea came home. Isobel heard Hosea's buggy and went out to meet him. She was too late, though. He had already gotten out of the buggy and was speaking with Travis and Emma.

Isobel walked toward them.

Hosea grabbed Isobel's hand. "Isobel, it is you, isn't it? I thought my wife had left me for another man when I saw these two together."

They all laughed.

"*Jah*, it's me," Isobel said. She was at least a little pleased that he pretended he had affection for her in front

CHAPTER 37

of others because when they were alone, he was so distant.

"We must be getting back now. It was nice to see you again, Hosea," Emma said.

"It was nice to see you again and nice to meet you, Travis," Hosea said.

"I'll just say goodbye to *Mammi*." Emma walked toward the house. She didn't know how to talk with Isobel about their father. Perhaps it was better said in a letter.

"Come and have another cup of tea and you can tell Hosea the *gut* news," Isobel urged.

"*Jah*, do stay, Emma. I haven't seen you for some time. I'll just put the horse away," Hosea said.

Emma and Travis looked at each other, and Travis gave her a nod, and then Emma said, "Okay, we can stay a little longer."

As they all sat around the table, Emma said, "The news is that Travis is getting a job close by to here next year. It's in Parkesburg."

"I thought that you might say that you're getting married." Hosea laughed. "Congratulations on the job." He put his hand out to shake Travis's hand. "That is good news."

"Thank you." Travis laughed. "No, we're not getting married."

Isobel noticed that Emma smiled at Travis adoringly, and he gave a little look back at her, which made her envious. If only Hosea would look at her like that.

As they finished the last of their tea, Emma summoned

up some courage to talk about their father. "I wonder if we can speak again in private for a moment, Isobel."

Isobel nodded, and the two girls walked outside onto the porch. "What is it, Emma? Haven't we said all there is to say?"

"There was something that I wasn't going to mention to you, but I think you should know. I told *Mammi* just now. I haven't told you yet because it's awful to speak of."

Isobel knew from the look on Emma's face that what she was about to say was extremely important. She held her breath and said, "Yes?"

"It's about our father."

That was the last thing that she thought Emma would speak about. "Go on."

Emma stared into her face as if she was searching for answers. "Do you know who he is?"

Isobel nodded. "Yes, kind of. I kind of know who he is by name only. So, did you find out?"

"Yes, I found our birth certificates in Mom's paperwork."

"*Jah*, that's how I found out. It was the man she used to work for. Mom doesn't know that I found out."

"Well, she knows that I know," Emma said. "She discovered me in her bedroom when I was going through her papers."

"Oh, that wouldn't have been good." Isobel held her stomach as she always did when she was nervous. "What excuse did she give you about the affair?"

CHAPTER 37

"Affair? No, there was no affair or anything of the sort." Emma told her what had happened.

Isobel gasped, and her stomach flip-flopped. "How horrible. I never ever even thought of something like that. All this time, I imagined our father to be someone good, someone interesting, someone we'd want to meet, but the truth is awful."

"It's awful, all right. It's dreadful thinking of that happening to any woman, and it's also awful to think that's how we came into the world."

"Poor Mom." Isobel could not even think of that terrible thing happening to her. It was bad enough that her mother was all alone and then found out that she was having two babies and not one.

"Yeah, she was very upset to tell me about it. That's why she's kept it a secret all these years. She had no support, so she had to give one of us away."

"He should be in jail, Emma. Even though it happened years ago, he can still be charged with assault. That's what we should do."

"I have given it a lot of thought. I don't think that would be a good idea. He's got family, and it would affect them as well."

"What if he does it again? Maybe he has done it before and maybe since."

Emma shook her head and put her hand to her forehead. "I think Mom just wants to forget it. She hasn't done anything all these years, so I'd say she wants to forget about it."

CHAPTER 37

"*Nee,* that would be the very thing people like that count on. They're cowards and like to intimidate people into keeping quiet."

"Well, it's up to her whether she wants to go through all that," Emma said.

Isobel fiddled with the strings on her prayer *kapp* while she wondered what purpose *Gott* would possibly have in the situation. Maybe some good would come of it. "Poor Mom. I had no idea, no idea at all."

"Well, it seems as if *Gott* wanted us to come into the world."

Isobel shook her head. "Horrible way to come into the world."

Emma stepped in and hugged Isobel. The last time they'd hugged was the first time they'd met. Back then, Emma had a bad feeling when she'd hugged her. Today, Emma felt the hug from her twin was genuine. The issue about their father had brought them closer.

"I'm glad you came, Emma. Let's both be friends, as twins should be."

"*Jah,* I'd like that. We have to stick together."

CHAPTER 38

Weeks had gone by since Emma and Travis visited Isobel, and Emma was satisfied that Travis was well and truly over the feelings he once had for her twin sister.

Seeing Isobel had been good for her too, and she believed that *Gott* was healing her heart. She forgave Isobel for what she'd done. She was also able to fully forgive her mother once she'd learned the true circumstances of why she'd abandoned her.

Travis played tennis every Tuesday night, and sometimes Emma went along to watch. Emma was invited to play but always declined, as she much preferred to watch. The only sport Emma had ever played growing up in the Amish community was volleyball.

The tennis games were never serious, but Travis did become quite competitive in a friendly way. Emma admired his drive to win; he was like that with everything he did and always put the best of his ability into it.

CHAPTER 38

After tennis, they would have a meal somewhere before Travis took her home. While she waited for him to have a shower, Emma thought about the time that Travis told her he loved her and then kissed her. She wondered if she had missed an opportunity. It had been a perfect time for her to say that she loved him too.

Now things were just awkward. She couldn't blurt out that she loved him. She hoped that another moment like that one would come along soon.

Once Travis joined her, they decided to take a walk to the diner down the street.

As they sat down and looked through the menu, Travis said, "Come with me, Emma."

"Come with you to where?"

"Come with me to Parkesburg. There's nothing keeping you here, and I can't even think of my life without you in it." Travis lunged for her hand and held it tightly. "Marry me?"

"Really?"

"Yes, I want you to marry me. You've become like a part of me, a part of my heart. I don't ever want to be without you."

"This is quite sudden." Emma looked from side to side, hoping that no one could overhear their conversation. "I need to think about it."

"I hope you say 'yes.' Of course, you must think about it if you feel you need to."

Right now, Travis was the only person that Emma could trust. She loved him, but did she love him enough?

CHAPTER 38

"I need time to sort out my feelings." She knew she did not want to be without him; she just wasn't sure that was a good enough reason to marry him.

After the waitress had taken their order, Emma said, "Travis, I think I can't make plans for my life until this thing with my father is sorted out." Emma was mixed up about so many things. She was forced out of her Amish life and was too humiliated to return. Neither did she feel comfortable amongst the English. Maybe the key to her life would come through her father and finding out more about him. Perhaps he had a side to his story. Could her mother have exaggerated what happened?

"Sorted out in what way?"

"I'm not sure, but I need some kind of ending to it."

"Is there anything I can do to help?"

Emma picked up a glass of water and swallowed a mouthful. "Yes, you could drive me down to speak to Isobel again if you could. I think it's something the both of us need to talk about."

Travis tipped his head slightly to the side. "Again? You just saw her. Can you call her?"

Emma just looked at him with the best pleading expression on her face that she could muster until he said, "Okay. You just name the day, and I'll rearrange my work schedule."

The waitress placed their burgers on the table and then left.

"What is it that you're searching for, Emma?"

CHAPTER 38

"The truth. They say there are two sides. I've heard one side. I need to hear the other."

"That doesn't make sense." Travis moved uncomfortably in his seat. "Do you feel incomplete without meeting your father?"

"I think so. If I found out more about him, then I might be able to move forward with my life. I don't even know what he looks like in person or even what his voice sounds like. These are things I need to know. I keep thinking if I wait too long, he might die and then it'll be too late. I don't want to live with regrets."

Travis nodded and looked down at his drink.

"I'm sorry that I've been a little stressed lately," Emma added.

Travis gave a smile that revealed his handsome white teeth. "You've been through a lot. Don't give it another thought. I'll do whatever I can to help you."

"Can we see Isobel tomorrow?"

Travis laughed. "I didn't expect you meant that soon, but okay. I've got a few things on, but I can re-schedule them."

"Good. The sooner we get moving on this, the better."

"Anything to make you happy."

"I'd like you to find out about my father tonight on the Internet. I want to learn every detail."

"Okay." Travis nodded. "I'll see what I can find out."

"Good. You can tell me all about what you learn on the way to see Isobel tomorrow."

CHAPTER 39

When Travis and Emma knocked on the door of Emma's old house, they found out that Isobel was the only one at home. The two girls left Travis in the house while they went for a walk in the fields.

The air was cool and crisp, and the only sounds were the rustling of leaves and the occasional chirping of birds.

Suddenly, Emma stopped and turned to Isobel. "I have to tell you something," she said, her voice barely above a whisper.

Isobel looked at her twin, concern etched on her face. "What is it?"

Emma took a deep breath and looked down at her feet. "I'm in love with Travis," she said, her voice barely audible.

"I know that. I'm not a fool."

"Do you approve?"

"I do."

Emma was relieved. They kept walking, the tension

CHAPTER 39

between Emma and Isobel dissipating with each step. They approached a secluded area of the fields, a place that Emma had always enjoyed as a child. It was a small hill surrounded by wildflowers.

Emma cleared her throat. "Isobel, I'm here because I have an idea."

"About what?"

"I think we should confront our father over what he did to our mother. I want to know what he's got to say about it."

Isobel held her stomach. *"Nee,* I couldn't do that."

"You must come with me. I'm going to do it with or without you. Travis had a look on the Internet and found out where he works. He also found a photo of him."

"Where did he find the photo?"

"On the Internet. He printed it out." Emma opened her bag that was slung around her shoulder and pulled out a book. She opened the book, and inside was a picture of their father.

Isobel took it and studied it. The photo was only black and white but that didn't matter. "That's our father? He doesn't look anything like us. I guess he's a man, and we're women, but I thought he'd have similar features."

Emma nodded. "Well, that's him all right."

Isobel handed back the photo.

"I say we wait outside of where he works rather than go to his home. That way we won't upset his family."

"I guess that would be better. When do you think we

CHAPTER 39

should do this? And what do you expect him to say?" Isobel asked.

Emma shrugged her shoulders. "I just want some kind of explanation, some sort of... well, he could say that he's sorry for how he treated our mother."

"I don't think it's a good idea, but if you're determined to go through with it, I'll come with you." Isobel sighed.

"You will?"

Isobel nodded.

"We'll do it tomorrow."

Isobel gasped and held her throat. "Tomorrow? That's so soon."

"*Jah* or we'll have too much time to think about it and too much time to find reasons not to do it." Emma was a little surprised to hear herself being so forthright and decisive. "I can talk Travis into us staying overnight somewhere close, and we'll come first thing in the morning and pick you up and drop you back tomorrow night."

"Okay." Isobel took a deep breath, stopped walking, and Emma stopped too. "Emma, I just want to say to you again that I'm sorry. I'm sorry for marrying Hosea and not telling you. I'm sorry for not telling you when I developed feelings for him. I know that you liked him very much, and I just disregarded that." She stared intently into Emma's face. "Can you forgive me?"

"You've already asked me to forgive you. You don't need to ask twice. Yes, I forgive you." Emma smiled and patted her shoulder.

CHAPTER 39

"*Denke.*" Isobel looked into the distance. "I feel much better now."

"I'm glad."

When they got back to the house, Travis and Emma declined the invitation to stay for dinner, preferring to relax at a local B&B.

After Travis had booked their rooms, they went for a drive to find somewhere to eat.

"I think I'm going to like living around here. The air is so clean," Travis said.

"That's one of the things I miss about being here. The air is so different from New York."

"Are you sure that you want to go through with all this, Emma?"

Emma gave a little grunt. "No, I'm not sure, but I'm going to do it. So don't ask me again."

"All right, I won't."

∼

The very next morning, when Emma and Travis called for Isobel, they were surprised to see her in *English* clothes. "Isobel, you're not wearing your prayer *kapp* or anything."

"We want to blend into our surroundings before we surprise our father. An Amish woman would attract too much attention."

Emma couldn't help but ask, "And what did Hosea say about that?"

Isobel giggled. "He already left for work, and no doubt

CHAPTER 39

it'll be late before we get back, and he'll be asleep. He knows I'm going though, of course."

As they walked toward the car, Isobel felt a sense of freedom wash over her as she walked in her tight-fitting jeans and a sleeveless top. It was a stark contrast to the long dresses and aprons she was used to wearing.

After a long drive back to New York, Travis parked his car close to the office building where the twins' father worked. "Are you sure you want to do this? I didn't know this is what you two were planning until this morning."

"I'm sorry that I didn't tell you everything," Emma said. "But we have to do this."

"I'll most likely stay in the car, but if I'm not here when you get back, just call me. I won't be far away."

"Okay," Emma said.

Travis couldn't help but feel uneasy about the situation. But he knew the twins were strong-willed and wouldn't back down. He decided to stay close by in case anything went wrong.

As Emma left the car, the weight of her decision began to sink in. She was going to confront the man who had shattered her family and left her mother to pick up the pieces. With each step they took, Emma felt the anger and resentment toward her father build. She knew what they were about to do was risky, but it was the only way to find out the truth about their father.

Travis waited for a few minutes before getting out of the car. He paced up and down, trying to shake off the feeling of unease that had settled in his stomach.

CHAPTER 39

Isobel glanced over at Emma. "Well, what time do you think he'd finish work? How are we going to find him amongst crowds of people? Look. There are already lots of people coming and going."

"We'll have to think of something. I'm not going to come all this way for nothing." Emma was silent for a moment. "We could call his office and make an appointment to see him."

"What do you mean? As someone else?"

Emma scratched her head. "I guess that wouldn't work. Should we say that we are the press or the police?"

"I guess if we say we're either of those, he'd see us on short notice. *Nee*, I say we wait outside the building and take our chances. If *Gott* wants us to meet him, we will," Isobel said.

Emma thought it ironic to hear Isobel speaking about *Gott*, but she had to believe that she had changed. "Okay, if you're sure that's how you want to do it."

"I do."

"Everyone finishes at five. So let's come back a little before five, and we'll wait," Emma said.

"Look! Is that him?" Isobel pulled on Emma's arm.

Emma retrieved the crumpled photo out of her bag and glanced down at it. "Yes, I think so. I'm sure it's him."

"Let's go." Isobel strode off in front of Emma, and she caught up to her father. "Excuse me."

He turned around.

"Are you Kelvin Young?" Isobel asked.

CHAPTER 39

He looked at Isobel and then looked at Emma. "Yes, and you are?"

"We are Rose Byler's children."

Kelvin Young stared at Emma and Isobel incredulously. For a moment, he said nothing, just stared at them. Then, slowly, he spoke. "Rose Byler's children?" he repeated, as if the words didn't make sense to him.

"Yes," Emma said, her voice shaking with emotion. "We've come a long way to see you."

Kelvin's expression didn't change. "I don't know what you want from me," he said flatly.

"We want answers," Isobel said, her voice surprisingly strong. "We want to know why you left us. Why you left our mother to raise us on her own."

Kelvin's eyes flickered with something that might have been remorse, but it was gone so quickly that Emma couldn't be sure she'd really seen it.

He looked more closely at the two of them, and his face did not register any sign of recognition. "My old housekeeper, Rose Byler?"

The two girls nodded.

"What's this about? I haven't heard from her in a long time. How is she?"

"She's fine now that she's gotten away from you." Isobel had blurted out her words causing Emma to dig her in the ribs.

Kelvin Young took a step backward. "What do you want?"

CHAPTER 39

Isobel took a small step toward him. "We know what you did to her."

He studied the two girls. "I think I know what you're talking about. I couldn't have her work for me if she had two babies. I only had room for one; I was willing to give her an excellent reference. I'm sorry, but what could I do if I didn't have the room? I'm not a millionaire; I was struggling to pay her wage to begin with, and I was nice enough to make room for a baby as well."

"We're not talking about making her give one of us up." Emma's tone was stern.

"Now, look here. I did *not* make her give one of you up. It's a simple matter of accommodation. I could have gotten her a job elsewhere if she wanted to keep the two of you. The choice was entirely hers."

The two girls looked at each other, then Isobel said, "We're talking about you being our father."

∽

A look of shock covered the man's face. "That's a slanderous allegation. I've got a good mind to call the police. Are you trying to extort money from me with these outlandish accusations?"

Isobel continued, "We just wanted to meet you and see if you had some sort of excuse or reason for the horrid thing you did to our mother."

"No. There is no excuse for something like that. What my sister means is... we just wanted you to know we think you're an awful person and should be behind bars."

"Now listen. Someone's lied to you. I'm willing to do a paternity test if you wish, but I can tell you now that I am categorically not your father. It's simply not possible!"

The two girls looked at each other in shocked silence. Could he be telling the truth?

"You girls are making a big mistake. What made you think I'm your father?"

Emma studied his face to see if she could recognize any features. "You are named on our birth certificates."

"What? That's ludicrous. Give me your phone numbers. I'm going to contact my lawyer and get this thing sorted out."

After they had exchanged phone numbers, Isobel said, "Do you know if our mother was dating anyone back then?"

He looked up to the sky and tipped his head up slightly. "I seem to remember a tall, gangly-looking fellow who looked a bit Italian. It was many years ago, though, and I don't get involved in the lives of house staff."

"We're sorry," Isobel said.

He simply pursed his lips and walked away, leaving the twins standing there watching until he disappeared.

"Well, that was a bad idea. Poor man," Isobel said, shaking her head.

"I'm so shocked that Mom lied to us. How could she lie to us so blatantly about something so important? Why would she put his name down as our father?"

CHAPTER 39

Isobel was still shaking her head. "I'm speechless about the whole thing, just speechless. I have no answers."

"Well, I don't know about you, but I'm hurt that she lied to us." Emma sighed heavily. "At least now we know we didn't come into the world the way she said. We still don't know who our father is, though."

"Yeah, we're back to square one."

Emma took out the photo she had in her bag, looked at it, and pushed it back into her bag. "Could it be Frank that Mom was dating back then? He said a tall, gangly-looking fellow. Frank's Italian, isn't he? He's tall, and years ago, he might have been gangly."

"Mom's only been with him ten years or so. Unless she knew him back then, and they came back together ten years ago," Isobel said.

"I wonder if she'll tell us the truth now that we've spoken with him."

"She won't be too happy with us. She might be sued or something for putting him on the birth certificate." Isobel bit her lip.

"Well, whatever happens, we're one step closer to finding out who our real father is." Emma linked her arm through Isobel's as they walked back to the car.

"*Jah*, but do we want to know? It just keeps getting worse the more we dig, doesn't it?" Isobel let out a deep breath.

"I'd rather know the truth, though, wouldn't you?"

"I suppose it would be good to know where we came

from. Frank's never seemed too interested in me, so I doubt that he's our father," Isobel said.

Emma squinted from the bright sunlight, and as she did, she wondered what would drive her mother to falsify a legal document. "This means that Mom not only lied to us, but she also lied on our birth certificates. That must be a serious offense."

Isobel nodded in agreement. "*Jah*, I suppose it would be. What shall we do? Shall we ask her about it?"

"We'll have to now. We'll have to because Kelvin Young's lawyer will be contacting her shortly, I'd say."

Isobel's brow furrowed as they rounded the corner and saw Travis's car. "I told Hosea and *Mammi* I'd be a little late, but I'd like a little time with Hosea before he goes to sleep. I must tell him about all this."

"Of course. We'll take you home now. No good ever comes from keeping secrets."

"*Jah*, I've learned that the hard way," Isobel said.

Travis saw the twins walking toward the car. He could tell things hadn't gone well. Isobel looked angry, and Emma had tears in her eyes. Travis immediately got out of the car and rushed to their side.

CHAPTER 40

When Isobel walked through the door of her home, Hosea was nowhere to be seen. She knew he was most likely already fast asleep. *Mammi* was still awake, sewing in the living room.

Mammi peered up at her through her thin-rimmed spectacles that sat low on her nose. "There you are."

"*Jah*, we went to New York. I've got to tell you something." Isobel had to tell someone. "Emma said she told you about our father."

"*Jah*."

"Well, it turns out that we don't think it happened like that."

"Why's that? Tell me everything, Isobel. Don't try and hide things from me just because I'm old."

"Okay. The truth is that we went to see the man who is named on our birth certificates. He was shocked and said

CHAPTER 40

he would see his lawyer, and he even offered to get a paternity test done. He isn't our father."

"Hmm. Isobel, what do you hope to achieve by all this digging that you're doing?"

"I want to know where I came from, and so does Emma. Don't we deserve to know who our father is?"

"Isn't it more important to know where you are and where you're going? What does it matter where you came from? Can you change the past?"

Isobel shook her head.

"So why pay it any mind?"

Isobel shrugged her shoulders. The way *Mammi* said things always made sense. Maybe it didn't matter where they had come from, but it irked her to know her mother had lied through her teeth about the whole thing. "Why would Mom lie, though? I just want things to make sense."

"People lie all the time. It's not something that's uncommon. She had her reasons, don't you think? She might've been trying to save you from pain."

"You know who your parents were, don't you?" Isobel asked.

"*Jah*, I do."

"I don't mean to sound rude or disrespectful, *Mammi*, but if you hadn't known them or one of them, you might be feeling how I'm feeling now."

"Very possibly." *Mammi* folded her sewing and placed it in the side cabinet. "Now it's time for an old lady to go to bed. *Good night.*"

CHAPTER 40

"Night, *Mammi*."

That night, Isobel could not sleep as different scenarios ran through her mind about why her mother lied on their birth certificates. Why hadn't her mother just put down that the father was unknown if she didn't want the truth to be told?

Had she planned on extorting money from Mr. Young with her lies at some point? Her mother hadn't always lived a comfortable life, so maybe she was hedging her bets.

Nothing Isobel could think of made sense to her. She would just have to hope that her mother would tell Emma the truth about the situation.

As Isobel tossed and turned in bed, she couldn't help but feel like she was missing a crucial piece of the puzzle. She knew that finding out who their real father was wouldn't change anything that had happened in the past, but it would give her and Emma a sense of closure. She needed to know why her mother felt the need to lie all these years.

~

Emma should have been lying awake thinking about Travis and him wanting to marry her, but instead, she was thinking of her mother, who her father was, and why there were lies on her birth documents.

Emma's mind raced as she tried to come up with possible reasons for her mother's deception. Did she have

CHAPTER 40

an affair with another married man? Was their father someone dangerous? Or was it simply a case of shame and embarrassment?

She needed answers, and the only person who could give them to her was her mother. Emma knew that she had to confront her mother about the lies, but the thought made her anxious. She didn't want to hurt her mother, but she needed to know the truth.

The next day, Emma made a special lunch for her mother and herself again. She pretended she wanted to discuss her career options, but she really wanted to discuss Kelvin Young and her real dad.

Once they were seated with their lunch in front of them, it was her mother who spoke first. "So, Emma. What have you been thinking about doing with yourself? Do you think you should get your GED? It'll be hard to get a decent job without it unless you want Frank to find you one."

"Mom, I really don't want to talk about that. I can't really think about doing anything with my life until something else is sorted out."

Her mother swallowed what was in her mouth and said, "What's that?"

"My father."

She rolled her eyes. "What of him?"

"Promise you won't get mad if I tell you something?"

"Emma, what did you do?"

"Isobel and I went to see Kelvin Young."

CHAPTER 40

Her mother gasped and dropped her fork onto the table. "Why?"

"Thing is, Mom, he denies everything. We know he's not our father, and we want you to tell us who he is."

"He denied it? Well, he's not going to admit it. What were the two of you thinking? Where did you see him?" Her hand trembled as she spoke. "Stay away from him!"

"We saw him outside of his work. Anyway, that doesn't matter. We know he isn't our father." Emma did not want to upset her, but she needed the truth, and this was the only way she knew how to get it.

"He *is* your father. Why would I lie?"

"We know he was telling us the truth. He even offered to have a paternity test."

"You don't believe me, and you believe a total stranger, the stranger who took advantage of me?"

"It's not that we believe him over you. It's just that he looked shocked and didn't know what we were talking about. We had to explain things to him."

"Did it occur to you that he's just a very good liar?"

"He was convincing." Emma frowned, not knowing who to believe.

"I promise you on everything that I love that, that man – Kelvin Young, is the father of both you and Isobel. There is no other possible father."

Emma blew out a deep breath. "Sorry, Mom. He was so convincing and was so outraged and even called you 'house staff' or 'housekeeping' or something like that. He even said that you were dating a tall, Italian-looking man."

CHAPTER 40

Her mother shook her head. "I was not dating anyone. I never even dated a man until after you girls were born. He was lying."

Emma shook her head in disgust at the terrible man. "Why didn't you go to the police?"

"It was easier just to carry on with my life than answer a whole barrage of embarrassing questions and have probing examinations. I just couldn't go through with all that. I would have lost my job, and I had no money. I couldn't go back to the community; I just couldn't."

Emma nodded. She knew what it was like – not being able to go back to the community. The embarrassment of trying to stop Isobel and Hosea's wedding was enough to make Emma never want to go back to the community. "I'm sorry I doubted you, Mom."

Her mother wiped a tear away from her eye. "Do you see now why I didn't report him?"

"I guess so."

As soon as they finished lunch, Emma called Isobel to tell her what she had learned. Emma had to be careful to phone Isobel at mealtimes. That way, Isobel would be in the kitchen and able to hear the phone in the barn.

"Well of course she would say that, Emma. You're so gullible sometimes," Isobel told her.

"But she seemed to be telling the truth." Emma was confused, she believed her mother, but she also believed Kelvin Young when he stood in front of her.

Isobel said, "The trouble with you is that you believe everything anyone tells you."

CHAPTER 40

"Well, who do you believe? Why would she put his name on the birth certificates, then?"

"Who knows why she would do that? She probably didn't want to put our real father's name on it. I believe Kelvin Young. He seemed genuinely shocked," Isobel said.

"Why haven't we heard from his lawyer yet?" Emma was a little taken aback that Isobel still believed Kelvin Young over their mother.

"These things take time. They're probably doing their research to support their case. They'll need evidence–facts."

"I see. Travis says that we should both get DNA tested," Emma said.

Isobel giggled. "To prove we're sisters? I don't think we need to do that."

"No, not for that. To get our DNA just in case we need it for later. There might be a court case."

"I'll do that as soon as I can."

"I've got an appointment tomorrow to get it done. I guess it's a good idea in case Kelvin is going to get a lawyer involved."

"Okay, I'll book in to get one done, too," Isobel said. "There should be someplace around here that does it."

"Have you told Hosea of all this?" Emma asked.

"Hosea seems to have a lot on his mind lately. I don't want to bother him. I intend to tell him about the whole thing. I will soon."

CHAPTER 40

When Isobel got off the phone from Emma, she stared at the phone in the barn as she considered how strange it was to be living where Emma had once lived, and now Emma was living with her mother and Frank. They had traded places for real.

The worst thing was that she did not know how to win back Hosea's interest.

Isobel wished she could share her deepest concerns with him, but she did not feel connected with him as Emma obviously had connected with Travis. How different would her life be if she was close to Hosea like that?

Isobel sighed deeply and leaned against the barn wall, lost in thought. She knew that she had to do something to reignite their passion, but she did not know what to do.

Hosea had been distant lately, and she could not help but feel that it was partly her fault. She had been too focused on herself and her problems, and she had not paid enough attention to him.

Their relationship had become stagnant, and she had not taken the time to try and fix it. But now, with the possibility of a court case looming, Isobel knew that she needed Hosea more than ever. She could not face Kelvin Young alone.

She took a deep breath and decided to talk to Hosea as soon as he got home from work. She would tell him everything that had happened with Kelvin Young and her doubts about their mother's story. She would be open and honest with him, and would listen to what he had to say. Maybe they could figure out a way to face this together.

CHAPTER 40

As Isobel waited for Hosea to come home, she replayed the conversation with Emma in her head. She knew that Emma had believed their mother, but now both of them doubted her. Kelvin Young had seemed so genuine, so sincere. She couldn't shake the feeling that he was telling the truth.

Finally, she heard Hosea's horse and buggy pulling into the driveway. She took another deep breath and walked out to meet him.

"Hey there," he said, giving her a quick kiss before heading back to tend to his horse.

"Can we talk for a minute?" Isobel asked, following him.

"Sure, what's up?"

Isobel sighed and began her tale about Kelvin Young and the story of their mother, including Emma's decision to take a DNA test. Hosea listened quietly with a grave expression as she spoke.

Eventually, he concluded that it was best for Isobel to take the same test and discover the truth. He pulled her close to him, assuring her that no matter what happened, everything would turn out alright.

CHAPTER 41

Travis and Emma kept up their ritual of going to dinner with each other three times a week. Once they were seated at the restaurant, Emma looked over at him.

He was smiling from ear to ear. The candlelight danced around, lighting up his face with a red hue.

"What is it? You've been acting strangely since you picked me up."

Travis reached across the table with his hand, and Emma reciprocated. Their hands touched and locked together. Emma felt soothed by the warmth he offered.

"I've done something. I hope you won't be angry with me," Travis said.

"Depends on what it is."

"I've been stalking Kelvin Young."

Emma pulled her hand away in shock, mouth ajar. "What did you say?"

CHAPTER 41

"Following him around to try and get a DNA sample from him. I finally got it."

"Oh my gosh! How did you manage that?"

"I followed him on Friday night and collected the glass he drank out of. Thankfully, that was enough for a sample."

Suddenly Emma felt like she had stumbled into one of those detective novels she'd found in Isobel's apartment. "Really? How do you know?"

"I gave it to Damian, a friend of mine who has some knowledge in forensics."

Emma shook her head in disbelief. "You shouldn't have. You were risking being seen. What if Kelvin Young had caught you taking his glass?"

Travis snickered. "I don't know if there's a law about trying to get a DNA sample. Maybe there is."

"Still, you should have thought twice. What do we do next?"

Travis reached for Emma's hand again across the table. "We need to compare the test results from you and Isobel with Kelvin's results."

Emma smiled, placing her hand back into his. "Okay, can Damien assist us with this?"

"Yeah, he does that kind of work for a living. Close to it, anyway."

She pulled out her cell phone and called Isobel, getting through on the first try. She shared the news of their DNA testing and was told that Isobel would send the results soon so they could compare them with Kelvin's. After she

262

hung up her call, Emma looked at Travis with an inquisitive stare.

"What now?" He asked, "Why are you looking at me like that?"

A grin played on the edges of Emma's lips. "You've been so good to me. I'm grateful to have you in my life."

"I'd do anything for you, Emma – anything," Travis said.

Emma chuckled. "It appears so; it wouldn't have even crossed my mind that you would go to such lengths."

"Should we tell Rose what we're doing?"

"No. She insists he is our father. I don't want her to think I doubt her. And if the test shows that he's not our father, we have to know that she would've had a good reason to hide our real father's identity." Emma shrugged her shoulders.

"Emma, you're so sweet and unassuming."

"I'm not really like that." Emma remembered back to all the ugly thoughts she had about Isobel once upon a time. There was nothing sweet about those, and she knew for certain she had the capacity for bitterness when provoked. In the Amish world, she had been gentle until Isobel showed up and tested her patience greatly. "I really can't believe that you followed Kelvin Young."

Travis laughed. "Well, I did, and no one suspected a thing."

CHAPTER 41

It was twenty days later that Travis had the results of all their tests. He stopped by Emma's house to tell her.

They sat in the garden while he broke the news. "I have the results of the paternity test here in the envelope."

Emma looked at what Travis held in his hand. It looked like a plain manilla folder, and was sealed with a red sticker.

"Travis, I think what we've done must be illegal. I mean to have Kelvin's DNA tested without him knowing."

"I'd say it's highly likely that it is. You do want to know who your father is, though, don't you?"

"Yes, of course. Quick, tell me."

Travis laughed. "We'll worry about legalities later."

"Did Damien tell you the results? Do you already know?"

"No, I told him to put it all in the envelope along with an explanation in plain English, not in scientific mumbo jumbo. I thought that maybe you and Isobel would like to open it together."

"I'll ask her, but it's such a long drive."

"It's up to you. You could call her."

"Good idea."

It was on Emma's third consecutive call that Isobel answered the phone. Emma explained to Isobel why she called, then shut her eyes and sent up a quick, silent prayer to *Gott* that all would work out okay for everyone.

She opened her eyes and glanced at Travis, who gave her a nod and a wink. "Okay, Isobel, I'm opening the envelope right now."

CHAPTER 41

Travis retrieved a pocketknife, and with one slice the red sticker was in two pieces. A piece of paper floated to the ground. Travis leaned down and picked it up, and then handed it to Emma.

Emma took the paper from him and, looking down at her shaking hands, she tried to soften her breathing.

She scanned the paper in front of her and skipped to the bottom line. "The probability that sample A is the biological father is ninety-nine-point nine percent." Emma dropped the paper and looked at Travis. "So, he is our father?"

"Yes. That's what it says." Travis' jaw clenched.

"Mom was telling the truth. That liar," Isobel said.

Emma grabbed Travis' arm firmly. "He must be hoping we'll give up and not tell anyone what he did."

"I can't believe how he fooled me. I even believed that Mom was lying. I better go now, Emma—Hosea is just coming home. Tell Travis 'thank you' for all this, ok?"

"Will do. Bye, Isobel," Emma placed her cell phone on the table and then looked at Travis. "Now what are we going to do?"

"Does your mom want to let him get away with it?" Travis asked.

"She doesn't want anyone to know what happened to her. She won't change her mind."

"So you're just going to accept it and move on?" Travis asked.

"Yeah, I'm fine with knowing what really happened—that's all I wanted anyway. I want nothing to do with him,

CHAPTER 41

and he obviously doesn't want anything to do with us either."

Travis looked at Emma with disbelief. "You can't just let him walk away with what he did. He needs to face the consequences for his actions."

Emma sighed. "I know, but I can't force my mom to press charges. She's been through enough already, and it's her decision."

Travis stared at her for a moment before speaking, "Then we'll take matters into our own hands. We'll make sure he pays for what he did to your mom."

Emma looked at him, unsure of what he meant. "What are you suggesting?"

Travis leaned in closer, his dark eyes locked onto hers. "We'll make him regret ever laying a hand on her. We'll teach him a lesson he won't forget."

Emma's heart raced as she contemplated his words. She knew it was wrong, but the thought of revenge was tempting.

"No, Travis. I'm grateful to you for wanting to make things right, but what's done can't be undone. I have my mother and my sister. Now I've got you too and that's so much more than I had before. My heart is filled with love. If we do what you say, I fear that bitterness or hate will creep in."

"I understand. I just want to help."

"I know."

He grabbed her hand and squeezed it.

CHAPTER 42

After dinner that night, Travis and Emma went for a stroll through the streets.

"Emma, I don't mean to pressure you, but you know the truth about everything, are you ready to get married?"

Emma laughed. "Well, that's a romantic way to ask me again."

Travis smiled, got down on one knee, and took hold of her hand. He said under his breath, just loud enough for Emma to hear. "You had better say yes."

Emma waited for him to continue.

"Emma Byler, will you do me the honor of becoming my wife?"

After a moment of looking into his eyes, she said, "Yes, Travis, I will."

Travis smiled, jumped to his feet, and pulled Emma into his arms. "I'm glad you said yes." He moved his lips over hers and kissed her softly. "Are you sure you're

CHAPTER 42

ready? I don't want you to say later that I pressured you into it."

"I'm very sure. I'm ready to move on with my life, well, our life together."

From his pocket he produced a ring. It had small diamonds dotted all around it. He took her hand and slipped it onto her finger. "It's a symbol of our engagement. You can change it if you want. I wasn't sure what you'd like."

She stared down at the ring. "I love it. It's perfect."

"Are you sure? It's not flashy or anything."

"That's what I love about it," Emma said.

"On the weekend, let's drive down and find a place in Parkesburg, somewhere close to where I'll be working. Of course, we'll have to stop in and tell everyone the good news," Travis said.

"Let's all go. Mom and Frank too. When we're all at my grandmother's, we can tell everyone together."

"Sounds like a good idea." Travis chuckled.

There was one thing that Emma had to do first before they visited her grandmother, and that was talk to her mother and share what she had just learned. She was going to let things go, but something inside her made her want to tell her mother she knew the truth about her father and that she believed her.

Later that night, she asked her mother to come into the kitchen so that they could speak alone.

"What is it? You look troubled, Emma."

"Mom, I'm sorry that I didn't believe you about that

man being our father."

Her mom eyed her sceptically. "Do you believe me now?"

"We got him DNA tested."

"How did you get him to agree to that?" Her mother scrunched up her nose.

Emma told her everything.

"Well, I'm glad you know for sure, but you didn't have to go to all that trouble. You could just have believed me."

"I know. I feel sorry for not believing you. I did at first, but he was just so convincing when we spoke to him."

Rose sighed. "Yes, most liars are. That's why people believe them, so they just keep on lying."

Emma narrowed her eyes. "I wish he would be punished for what he did."

"Emma, I might not be Amish anymore, but one thing I've learned from them is that it is *Gott* who judges. It's not up to us."

"But what about the wife and his other children? Don't they have a right to know? I still don't think he should get away with it."

Her mother shrugged her shoulders. "Maybe his family should know, but who is it who has the right to tell them?"

Emma considered what her mother said while she stared into the distance. She did not want to be the one to tell them whether she had the right to or not. Would it be best to let things go? "I just find it hard to think about him getting away with what he did."

CHAPTER 42

"I know. I've lived with it for a long time. I'm just glad that you're back with me now. I have both my daughters and I'm never going to let you go." She leaned over and hugged Emma.

"You've been away from the Amish for so long, Mom, yet you speak as if you are still Amish."

"I've had to come to terms with what happened to me. I have my own relationship with *Gott*. Just because I've left the Amish does not mean that I have left *Gott*. I've always prayed for you."

Her mother's words gave Emma new respect for her. She was not selfish and uncaring as she had supposed. It meant everything that her mother had prayed for her. "I admire your faith, Mom."

Her mom smiled, and her eyes became a little misty. "I don't think I would have survived without it."

"Maybe you can teach me some things," Emma said. "I didn't think I was judgemental, but I was about so many things."

The two of them hugged again.

～

Days later, they were all gathered at *Mammi's* house for dinner. As soon as Emma had stepped into her childhood house, fond memories of the past flooded back — keeping a frog as a pet, the time she brought a piglet to bed when she was five, and all those winter nights when *Mammi* told stories by the fire.

CHAPTER 42

When everyone greeted each other, it felt like one big happy family. It didn't seem to matter that some were *Englishers* and others were Amish.

The table was already laid out with delicious food. After they finished their prayers, everyone dug in.

Emma cleared her throat. "I've brought everyone here tonight for a reason."

Her mother gasped and put her hands to her mouth. "I thought so."

With amusement ringing in her voice, Emma said, "I haven't said anything yet, Mom."

"I know, but…"

Travis stood up. "Perhaps I should speak."

Emma gave him a nod.

"Emma and I wanted everyone here together so that we could tell you all that Emma has agreed to marry me."

Rose stood up. "I knew it; I just knew it."

Her mother and her grandmother were quick to hug them both. Hosea and Frank shook Travis' hand and gave Emma a kiss on the cheek.

Isobel lingered in the back, and after all the congratulations were done, she spoke. "My two favorite people getting married- that's just *wunderbaar!*"

Emma wondered if Isobel was truly pleased for them or not. She hadn't rushed to congratulate them as the others had.

Isobel inquired, "Have your parents been told yet, Travis?"

"No, we'll tell them when we return tomorrow. Emma

CHAPTER 42

thought it best to break the news here first," he replied.

"So, you haven't even met his folks yet, Emma?" Isobel asked.

Emma squirmed nervously in her seat. She'd always evaded meeting his parents. "Not yet," she confessed.

"All in good time. They'll love her. I keep telling her that," Travis said, smiling at Emma.

"Did you find a place to live today?" Frank asked.

"Yes, we did. Hopefully, it will be for the two of us. It's just a B&B until we find something more permanent, but it's in the right area, and it's the right price. It'll do us until we find something more permanent."

"Oh yes, I didn't ask; when are you thinking of getting married?" Rose asked.

"Pretty soon; we don't want a big wedding or anything, just immediate family and a couple of our friends."

"Why not have it here?" *Mammi* asked.

"Oh, could we? I'd love that." Emma looked at Travis. "What do you think, Travis?"

Travis smiled and looked adoringly into her eyes. "Wherever you'd like."

"We can visit a lot too when we move here, Isobel. We're only about twenty miles from you. Travis is going to teach me to drive."

"*Wunderbaar,*" Isobel commented.

Now Emma knew that Isobel wasn't too thrilled with the news. Emma had to speak with her in private to see what was going on. After all, Isobel was married to Hosea, so she couldn't possibly be jealous of Travis, could she?

CHAPTER 43

Once the twins were alone, Isobel asked, "Are you trying to hurt me by marrying Travis?"

"No, Isobel. I'm in love with Travis."

"Really?"

Emma nodded. "Otherwise, I wouldn't have agreed to marry him."

"It seems too quick. Don't rush into anything."

The way Isobel's eyes flickered and looked away from her, Emma knew that she had meaning behind those words; they weren't just idle words that were said for no good reason. "What do you mean? You're happy, aren't you, Isobel?"

"Oh, yes. I'm very happy." Isobel smiled, but then her smile quickly faded. "I fear that Hosea has lost interest in me."

"No, that can't be true. I see the way he looks at you."

CHAPTER 43

"He seems cold toward me and not interested in me since the wedding. I think he's upset with me for not telling you that we were going to be married." Isobel sniffed as if she was about to start crying. "I lied to him."

Emma made a face. "You did?"

"*Jah*, and that's not any way to start a marriage or life in the Amish."

"Did you talk to the bishop about it?"

Isobel's gaze fell to the ground. "I had a talk to the bishop about me lying but not about Hosea's feelings toward me."

"What did he say?"

"The bishop's very easy to talk to. I explained everything, and he was very understanding."

"Well, that's good. Did you tell Hosea that you feel he's acting strangely toward you?"

"*Nee*, I just couldn't. He might speak of all the ways he's disappointed in me."

"No, Isobel. Surely you're just imagining all of this."

Isobel shook her head. "*Nee*, I'm not. He's cold, very cold toward me."

"Have your feelings toward him changed?" Emma asked.

"That's the problem. I'm even more in love with him as every day passes, but the problem is it also makes me more upset every day because I don't think he returns my love."

"You must tell him how you feel." Emma reached out and touched Isobel's hand. The last thing Emma thought she would be doing today would be counseling Isobel with marriage advice.

"Maybe I will. I can't live with this sadness."

"Yes, do it. Do it tonight."

"Emma, I thought that once I got married, I'd be happy forever. You know – happily ever after? Like the fairytales, but I'm not. I would be if Hosea acted differently toward me."

Emma smiled sympathetically, and Isobel leaned over and hugged her.

"*Denke* for listening to me, Emma. I feel better for talking to you."

"That's what twin sisters are for, isn't it?"

Isobel smiled. "For sure. We'd better get back, or they will think we're speaking about them."

Emma laughed and then the twins linked arms and walked back to the table where everyone was finishing off the desserts.

After the meal was finished, they sat in the living room in front of the fire.

"We'd better go soon," Rose said. "We'll stop by tomorrow morning before we leave. We're staying down the road, not far away."

"That'll be good, Mom," Isobel said.

Emma and Travis were also staying at the same B&B in separate rooms.

Emma stood up. "I'll help with the cleaning up before we leave."

"I'll help, too." Travis carried the dishes to the kitchen.

CHAPTER 43

Then he whispered to Emma, "You were gone for a long time. Is everything okay with Isobel?"

"*Jah*, she's fine. Just marriage teething problems, I'd say."

"Yikes, I hope we don't have any of those."

"Who knows, we might."

Travis glanced back at Isobel and Hosea, who were still sitting together. "Anyway, they seem to be happy enough now."

"They certainly do." Emma peered at Hosea. He seemed happy and content. Hopefully, Isobel was imagining problems where none really existed.

Frank looked up and saw Emma. "You and Travis come back over here. I have something to say, and this concerns everyone."

Emma hoped that Frank was not going to mention their biological father. Her mother had been upset enough, and Emma was sure she did not want any more talk of Kelvin Young.

Once everyone was seated, Frank stood up. "Now, don't get angry with me, Rose."

Rose smiled. "It depends on what you've got to say."

"I want to take this opportunity to ask you something, Rose. Will you be my wife?" Frank bent down in front of Rose and pulled a small box out of his pocket.

Rose's mouth fell open, and her hands flew to her face. "Frank, we've talked about this."

"Yes, we've talked about it, but we've never decided

CHAPTER 43

anything. I want to marry you soon and not on some far-off date in the future."

Frank glanced between Travis and Emma before stating, "I don't want to take anything away from this moment, but I don't know when or if we will all be together again."

"Yes! Of course! Yes, Frank, I will marry you!"

He stood up, and Rose sprung to her feet and threw her arms around him in an embrace. She then held out her hand, and he slid the ring onto her finger.

They all congratulated the happy couple.

"I knew you'd get married one day. It's about time." Isobel turned to *Mammi* and said, "Well, that only leaves you, *Mammi*. We'll have to find a man for you."

Mammi laughed. "I'm way too old and set in my ways."

Rose looked around at everyone. "I'm glad to have both my girls together at last. I want you both to promise me that you'll always be close, as twins should be."

Isobel looked at Emma and smiled. "We will."

"Yes, we will, Mom."

∽

Once everyone had gone home and the cleaning up was done, Isobel went to bed. Normally, she would climb into bed and try not to wake Hosea, who always went to bed earlier than she, but tonight she thought it was time to speak with him. "Hosea."

CHAPTER 43

"*Jah?*"

"Are you awake? I want to talk with you about something."

Hosea rolled around to face her and propped himself up on his elbow. "What is it?"

Isobel sat on the bed next to him. "I just feel that you have been distant with me. Are you disappointed that I lied about telling Emma and *Mamm* about the wedding?"

"*Nee*, I was a little shocked that you didn't tell them. But I wouldn't hold that against you and be upset with you. Is that what you think?"

Isobel sniffed back tears. "You've been distant with me."

"Don't cry." Hosea put his arm around her. "How have I been distant? I know I've been working hard so we can buy a house as soon as possible. Maybe I'm tired."

"Well, you don't seem the same now that we're married."

Hosea scratched his head. "I feel the same. I don't know that I'm acting any differently to you. I love you, Isobel. I love you just as much, no more – I love you more now than the day that we got married."

"You do?" Isobel asked.

"*Jah*, of course I do."

"Oh, Hosea." Isobel collapsed into Hosea's arms, grateful that her imagination had run away with her and grateful that Hosea really did love her, as she loved him.

"Forgive me that I haven't shown you that I love you or

haven't told you enough. I'll do better. I just figured you already knew since we're married." Hosea held her tightly. "I'm only new to marriage, you know. You must talk to me about things, Isobel. I want to make you happy, and if you aren't happy about something, I need to know."

"*Jah*, I will talk with you. I was just worried and thought that you deserved to be angry with me."

Hosea laughed. "If I'm ever angry with you, I'll let you know."

～

Emma was pleased that her mother and Frank would be married, and she hoped that Isobel and Hosea would work things out so they would be happy too.

Emma was pleased she had traded places with Isobel on her eighteenth birthday. It had worked out for all of them.

Mammi had been right; it had all happened for a reason, and *Gott* had brought someone into her life that was more suited to her than Hosea, and that man was Travis.

She had her twin back. Emma's life was filled with so much love and joy that she no longer felt like the unwanted twin.

Emma was wanted!

She was loved by her family, loved by Travis, and most of all, she was loved by *Gott*.

CHAPTER 43

Thank you for reading The Unwanted Amish Twin.

For more books by Samantha Price, head to:
www.SamanthaPriceAuthor.com

ABOUT SAMANTHA PRICE

Samantha Price is a USA Today bestselling and Kindle All Stars author of Amish romance books and cozy mysteries. She was raised Brethren and has a deep affinity for the Amish way of life, which she has explored extensively with over a decade of research.
She is mother to two pampered rescue cats, and a very spoiled staffy with separation issues.

www.SamanthaPriceAuthor.com

ALL SAMANTHA PRICE BOOK SERIES

Amish Maids Trilogy

Amish Love Blooms

Amish Misfits

The Amish Bonnet Sisters

Amish Women of Pleasant Valley

Ettie Smith Amish Mysteries

Amish Secret Widows' Society

Expectant Amish Widows

Seven Amish Bachelors

ALL SAMANTHA PRICE BOOK SERIES

Amish Foster Girls

Amish Brides

Amish Romance Secrets

Amish Christmas Books

Amish Wedding Season